Forget it

Claire Highton-Stevenson

DEDICATION

FOR THOSE WHOM WE CAN NEVER FORGET

ACKNOWLEDGMENTS

Without those who support us, who would we be?

Michelle Arnold

Team ItsClaStevOfficial:
Kim, Miira, Carol, Pam, Nic, Frankie, Mari.

My beautiful wife, Louise.
The friends who keep me grounded, while boosting my confidence
and encouraging me to live this dream!

And the guys and gals at Costa coffee, who keep me sufficiently
caffeinated while I write.

Prologue

She wants her.

It's that simple.

It's the only thought in her head as she stands at the bar watching her. The music is loud, loud enough to drown out any real thoughts of conversation, not that that it matters as she sips the last of her drink. The lights are colourful and bouncing around the walls like fireflies on a hot summer's night in the Bintan Island Mangroves in Indonesia, on a boat floating down the Sebung River. She'd spent a week there once on leave, back when the British Army made decisions for her time.

None of it matters now though. All of that feels like a lifetime away. Her attention is held; her future awaits.

Brooke Chambers has watched her from the moment she entered the club: the blonde that now sits by herself at a table for four, radiating elegance.

She's average in height, much like Brooke herself, but she wears heels that accentuate perfectly toned calves and give her an inch or two edge in stature. She was dressed for the office maybe, in a short black skirt that reaches just about the level of decency above her knees. There was something sexy about a woman of a certain age who knew how to dress herself well.

She's drinking a long glass of something colourful and filled with ice. The tendon and muscle in her arm flex as she lifts the glass to her mouth. Kissable lips just touch the rim of the glass as she takes a sip. She savours the flavour and then places the glass back down on the table, pushing it forward slightly with the tip of her index finger until it is safe and away from the edge.

As Brooke watches on, safe at her distance, the woman's friends begin to arrive and join her. Two men and three women. People that make Brooke jealous in an instant. She wants to be with them. In fact, no, she wants them to leave, to not exist and invade this private spectacle.

The woman laughs at something one of her friends has said and Brooke thinks it might be the sexiest thing she has ever seen.

The larger man of the two, the one who has been holding court for the last ten minutes, leans in and whispers something against her ear, and although the blonde is laughing, this time she doesn't look as though she is quite so comfortable with the group as Brooke first thought. She looks on edge, a little unnerved, anxious even, but she hides it well. She is there and yet, she is distant from them.

It sets her aside.

She stands out.

Her honey-coloured blonde hair flies around her face as her head whips one way and then the other, trying to keep up with the conversations. Sometimes she is successful; other times it's clear that she missed the joke. She falters, but still she smiles and keeps listening, and Brooke is enraptured even more. This woman exudes such confidence in the way that she dresses and takes in the world around her, and yet, it's all a façade with these people.

She has been blatant in her staring; several times the blonde has caught those dark, brooding eyes with her own surreptitious glance. Brooke blushed the first time, mainly out of politeness, but when Blondie smiled back at her the second time, Brooke was hooked even more.

Forget it

Sipping her drink, Brooke is watchful, alert to her every move. The woman glances over at her admirer and then heads to the dance floor, aware she is the object of someone's desire.

Watching her move was mesmerising, the way her body loosened to the beat. She looked relaxed and every inch the siren. Brooke wanted to devour her, let her hands roam over every inch of her there was to explore, and do it again, over and over. Her imagination raced at the endless possibilities, and positions she could have her in. Naked positions.

Brooke swallowed down her drink; a little Dutch courage never hurt. She checked her appearance in the mirror behind the bar. She looked good. Her hairstyle with the short back and sides was slowly growing out, the fringe flopping down over her eyes until she swept it back into place with her fingers. She was cute and she knew it. Not in an arrogant way, she could never be described as that, but she made the best of herself.

The game of cat-and-mouse flirting had gone on long enough. She wanted to talk with this woman. If she was lucky, she would be allowed to touch maybe, but as she placed her empty bottle down on the bar, ready to casually head on over and politely intrude on this little gathering, the reality hit her like a truck.

To Brooke's utter dismay, she was leaving.

Coats where shrugged on and bags grabbed from the floor. Drinks swallowed down in one last gulp as laughter erupted once more between them all.

A glance back at Brooke and then she was gone.

That was a week ago.

Chapter One

Brooke Chambers was a civilian now and for the first time in eight years, she was at a loss. An impasse. Eight years of loyal service to Queen and country had given her a sound grounding but now, life was pushing her in another direction; an important direction. She wasn't sure she was ready for something of this magnitude, but she was doing it anyway.

There had never been a plan to become a parent and yet here she was, an instant mother, of sorts.

Joining the army had been the job she had always wanted. Since she was a kid, it was all she had dreamed about doing, and had her choices been different six months ago, she probably wouldn't have left. But her personal circumstances had changed things rather rapidly, and the only option she'd had was to request a PVR.

A Premature Voluntary Release hadn't been the way she had ever foreseen her career ending. Her plans of promotion through the ranks and an early retirement were scuppered overnight, but she wasn't unhappy about it now. She couldn't be. Robin was far more important than rank.

Having a kid meant her savings were dwindling fast, not that there had been much to start with. It was only the payout of a small insurance policy from her dad that meant she'd had enough to set them up in the small 2-bed flat she had found. Moving out of the area and somewhere cheaper was out of the question right now. Robin was still at school; it didn't seem fair to disrupt that right now, not with exams coming up. So, Brooke had found a place that would work for them both, for now. It wasn't like her sister asked for much out of life.

Without a job though, things were getting tight, and moving could well be in the cards whether Robin liked it or not.

She wasn't used to sitting around in her spare time. Her days were spent with walks in the park and trips to the job centre, stopping by the library and wandering the shopping mall looking for vacancies. Applying for jobs was easy enough, but with so much competition, getting an interview was not quite so simple. So, she was overjoyed when the invitation to interview at Pollards Department Store in town came through. Without sounding arrogant, she was pretty sure that she could walk it. It was a good job, well-paying and steady. Robin had a school trip coming up, and that was going to cost a lot more than Brooke could afford without full-time employment. So timing was great.

Tonight though, Robin was staying over at her best friend Jasmine's again. The Khans had been good friends to Brooke and Robin, helping out when they could. Yasmeen, Mrs Khan, had been a godsend by having Robin stay a couple of times a week. She said that it was Jas begging and pleading, and how could she stand in the way of such friendship, but Brooke knew that it was also for Brooke, to give her time to herself to enjoy life and not just be a caregiver. In return, Jas stayed over at theirs a couple of times a week too. There were no set rules; the girls just picked a house to sleep in and that was that.

Now Brooke had a choice to make. A quiet night in watching nothing very much on TV, or prudently spending the £16.98 in her pocket on happy hour somewhere.

Bypassing her local pub was an impulsive decision. It was a ridiculous reason really, but Art felt like the place to head to, even if the chances of *her* being there were small. It didn't seem to matter how busy she kept herself; images of the woman kept infiltrating her thoughts at every inopportune moment. She kicked herself daily for not being a little quicker off the mark in introducing herself.

Art was in full swing at 6 p.m. most nights as the town's workforce made a quick stop before heading home after a hard day. Brooke pushed through the door, earning an appreciative glance from the female bouncer. It put a little spring in her step and she grinned back enthusiastically. Sidling up to the bar, she slipped a tenner out of her pocket, ready to take full advantage of the 2 for 1 deal they had going on; happy hour was her favourite time in any bar.

A casual glance around had already put her nerves at ease and filled her with disappointment all at the same time; the blonde wasn't here. Yet.

Catching the barman's attention, she ordered her drinks and silently said a prayer that the gorgeous blonde might turn up at some point.

There was, though, a painting on the wall that caught her eye, and she wandered over to examine it more closely. Two naked women entwined together inside a pint glass. She wasn't sure what it was meant to represent. Art was a simple thing for her. She either liked it or she didn't; she didn't need to understand it.

She swigged more of her drink and moved along to the next piece on the wall, swaying to the music as she studied it. She liked this song; it had been playing on the radio a lot lately.

Forget it

Oil on canvas.

Tilting her head one way and then the other, she still couldn't quite work it out. It was all swirls and colours that swept around each other in two circles. She liked it, but she didn't get it.

Her instincts felt the presence of someone standing behind her, just a few seconds before the aural confirmation.

"If you take a step back and look at it from a different angle, I think you'll *get* it." The voice was feminine and well-spoken. Sultry, a little breathy, and it came with a pleasing aroma that clung to Brooke's senses. Trusting a voice, she took a step backwards, moving closer against the warm body that didn't move away. She realised that what she wasn't seeing was the close up of a women's breasts.

"So I see." Brooke grinned, turning finally towards the owner of the voice and subsequent information. Honey blonde hair framing a confident, very attractive and familiar face: the blonde from last week. She felt her insides tumble and flip.

"I would ask if you'd like a drink, but I see you already have one." There was a slight twitch of her lip. Her eyes glanced down to the bottles in Brooke's hands before they rose slowly to find Brooke's dark and brooding orbs waiting. They found themselves locked in a battle of wills: who would look away first?

Brooke lost that battle. The overwhelming urge to look lower and check her out was undeniable. She was wearing the same heels, not too high but high enough to put them on the same level when she looked back up and found her eyes again piercing her very soul. Hazel green in colour, her eyes smiled when she did, tiny little laughter lines appeared at the corner. This close, she was simply stunning. She wore a simple black dress tonight. Muscular shoulders suggested that she swam, or worked out, maybe both. Not that it mattered to Brooke; there were plenty of exercise routines she could put her through in bed, she considered.

"Hi," she said, amused. It would seem that she enjoyed the appraisal and began one of her own.

Brooke couldn't help the grin that spread across her own face. "Hello," she replied casually, though she felt anything but, and took a swig from her lager to stop herself from blurting out something ridiculous, like *I love you*. She held up the bottle, which she was still yet to drink from, and offered it to the still-anonymous woman.

A manicured hand reached out and took it. She twisted it around and examined the label.

"Thank you." She must have approved because she brought it to her lips and took a mouthful, all the while keeping her eyes firmly on Brooke.

"I'm Brooke."

Slowly, she pulled the bottle from her mouth. Her tongue slid leisurely across her lips, collecting the moisture, the move ending with a delicate bite of the plump lower lip. "Catherine," she replied.

Brooke nodded. "Catherine." She let the name play over her tongue, sounded out the syllables and heard it repeat inside her head. It was a good name and it suited her. "Wanna get a seat and another drink?"

"Yes, I do." She winked and led the way.

Catherine was a lot of fun. She liked beer, but preferred wine. Chilean red if Brooke wanted to know, which she did; she wanted to know everything.

Catherine liked to dance, and go to the theatre, but she preferred a quiet night in with a good book if she was really honest. Her favourite authors were mystery writers and she loved a good detective story. She was a tea over coffee in the morning person, but she did enjoy an espresso in the afternoon to give her a little pick-me-up. She swam at the weekends and did a couple of yoga classes during the week, but mainly she was a sloth that preferred to relax and watch a movie.

Brooke told her about life in the army and how she was looking for work right now, but it wouldn't be long until she was employed again because she wasn't the type to sit around idly, and she was prepared to take just about anything if it meant she could pay her way. How she enjoyed sports and running. She loved chocolate, kebabs, and Chinese food, but not the kind from a take-away. She liked cooking her own from scratch.

She didn't mention Robin just yet.

"So, I wanna assume that you're single." Brooke flashed her that confident smirk that had done so well for her so far.

Catherine laughed and moved a little closer, playfully stroking a fingertip down Brooke's cheek. "Yes, very single."

Brooke tilted her head and sipped her colourful drink through a paper straw; they'd moved on from lager to something more interesting a while ago as happy hour had extended into a second and then third hour. "Well, I am sure that must be through choice." Catherine was maybe 10 – 15 years older than herself. Brooke was okay with that; older women held a certain experience and candour that girls her own age often lacked.

"I suppose it is, but that isn't to say that I wouldn't be interested, *if* the right person came along." She let her other palm slide along Brooke's thigh, the movement slow and questioning.

"Person?"

"Well, I prefer women, but I don't limit myself when needs must." Her voice was like silk, soft and sensuous. It wrapped around Brooke's senses like a gentle touch.

Brooke nodded, enjoying the warmth of the palm as it ghosted along her thigh and then came to a stop high enough up her leg to be almost indecent.

"Is that a problem?" Catherine asked, sipping her own drink. She sat back now, and Brooke instantly felt the loss.

She shook her head. "Oh, no, not at all...I guess I just made an assumption." She shrugged and took another sip of her drink. An errant piece of blonde hair hung loose and pulled her attention. She gently reached out and hooked it back behind Catherine's ear. It was incredible just how easy it was to talk to Catherine. Rarely did she feel this at ease with someone, especially a woman she was interested in, and she was entirely interested in Catherine. She was going to be braver this time. Licking her lips, her eyes darted to Catherine's mouth, and she imagined them soft and pliable, tugging against her own lips.

At twenty-six, Brooke was experienced enough. She knew what she liked and what she wanted, and right now, that was Catherine.

Forget it

They were on their 4th drink when Catherine made the bold move to kiss her. Conversation had continued, and with every opportunity they had gravitated closer to one another until the point that all Catherine had to do was lean in. She took her opportunity.

She didn't do this often. Mostly, she let them chase her long enough to get what she needed. She had noticed Brooke the previous week; couldn't fail to when the brooding dark eyes had spent all night watching her, and she was a little disappointed that she hadn't had the chance to get a closer look at her then. When she saw her again tonight checking out the artwork, she made sure not to lose out this time.

She wasn't disappointed so far.

The first kiss was surprisingly chaste. Brooke did not need any encouragement to enjoy the next one. Strong fingers slid easily into waves of soft hair until she and Catherine were but a breath apart still. "Sorry, I couldn't resist," Catherine uttered dreamily, enjoying the feeling of Brooke's fingers playing with her hair.

Leaning back in, Brooke smiled, whispering against soft lips, "Nothing to apologise for." She wanted to taste her, feel the warmth of her. Eagerly sliding her tongue inside Catherine's mouth, she wasted no time in taking the lead, probing and possessive, enjoying the sweetness of the alcohol on her tongue.

"I think I could kiss you all night if you let me." The hint of an invitation wouldn't hurt.

Catherine's lip twitched and her eyes sparkled as she glanced down shyly. Catching sight of her watch, she cursed. "Damn, it's nearly midnight, I need to get going. I have a huge meeting in the morning and I cannot be late."

Disappointment crushed her chest. "Maybe we can do this again sometime?" Brooke said hopefully, pulling out her phone, ready to ask for a number.

Smiling fully now, Catherine stood and pulled her jacket on. "I'd like that. Why don't you give me your number and I'll call you as soon as I have some time?"

Chapter Two

The kitchen table was a mess. Dirty plates with half-eaten toast were stacked up. Mugs of tea and glasses of juice scattered across it, interspersed with textbooks and pens. Robin hunched over her maths exercise book and frowned.

"How do you make so much mess in the mornings?" asked Brooke when she shuffled sleepily into the room. She scratched at her head and yanked at her vest top. The material was bunched up around her waist from a fidgety night's sleep.

"Did you get a job yet?" the fifteen-year-old snarked back.

"You already know I got an interview." She grinned, picking up the kettle. Water splashed at her as she filled it. "Did you get that form for me?"

Robin closed her book, put her pen in its case, and rolled her eyes at her sister. "Yeah, I left it by your bag on the sofa."

"Oh, right." She guzzled a glass of tap water while the kettle built up some steam. "I'll fill it out and you can take it in tomorrow."

"Whatever, I don't wanna go anyway." Robin shrugged as she pulled her long dark hair up into a ponytail. "We can't afford it," she said, opening her bag and shoving the books and pens inside.

Brooke sighed, a thin smile passing her lips. "Let me worry about that, okay. You're going on that trip. It will be good for you and you love history." The kettle boiled and she turned to pour the water into a clean mug.

"I can read it in books," she argued, pulling her school blazer on.

"That's not the same, Binni. This is going to be part of your exam and you know that Dad..." She felt her throat fill with emotion. "You know Dad wanted you to do well."

"Well, he isn't here, is he?" Robin said with a shrug. "He's dead, and Mum doesn't want to know."

Brooke shook her head. "That's not true."

"It is. And I know you wanna see the best in her Brooke, but I am done, she didn't even come to the funeral. You're all that matters to me now. You're the one that gave up everything for me. I'm gonna make you proud no matter what, Brooke."

She didn't remember ever being someone so prone to tearing up, but it was happening a lot for Brooke lately, especially where her younger sister was concerned. "You already do."

Robin tossed her bag over her shoulder. "It's just you and me now." Confirmation came with a gentle touch of her palm against Brooke's arm and a kiss against her cheek. "Get a job," she called out as she left.

Brooke watched from the window as Robin skipped down the short path that would lead to the pavement. Her eyes followed her all the way down the road to the corner, where Yasmeen Khan's car pulled up and Robin climbed in beside her best friend Jas.

Brooke turned back to the small table and blew out a breath. They really did need to get some kind of rota together. There was no way she was going to be able to live with this teenage mess for much longer. Checking her watch, it was 8.15 a.m. Three hours to get the flat shipshape and spotless before she would allow herself some fresh air.

But first, she would drink her tea. She grabbed her phone and flicked through a few apps. The news was miserable as usual. When she got to her text messages though, a small smile spread across her face.

She didn't recognise the number, but the message was clear.

Unknown number: Hi, this is Catherine. I am tied up all day today, but should be free this weekend.

Brooke smiled and fired off a reply.

Brooke: Hey, how does Saturday sound?

Chapter Three

80s music blared out from Brooke's room that Saturday afternoon. Her bed was covered in the clothes that she had tried on and then discarded.

She checked herself in the mirror for what felt like the hundredth time, pulling at the shirt she was hoping would work for her date tonight. Huffing, she grabbed the hem and ripped it off over her head, adding it to the pile before grabbing another from her wardrobe and pulling it on.

She was about to rip this one off too when the music from the radio was turned down. Turning, she found Robin in the room. "Got a date?" she asked, smiling at her big sister.

Coyishly, Brooke nodded. "Yeah."

Robin sat down on the edge of the bed. "You should wear that one," she said, denoting the tartan design Brooke now wore.

"Ya think? I dunno, she's kind of classy."

Robin raised a brow and laughed.

"What?" Brooke grinned. "I can do classy." She turned back to the mirror and grimaced. "You really think I should wear this?"

Robin nodded. "Yep, you look cute." She jumped up from the bed. "I'm going over to Jas's. Mrs Khan is cooking chickpea curry and I have dibs on a bowlful."

"Damn, I always miss out." Brooke joked. "I'll pick you up tomorrow at 11."

Forget it

"Alright." she leant in and kissed Brooke's cheek. "But don't come home early on my accord." The smirk she gave was just like their dad looking back at her. "You might as well enjoy yourself, and don't forget you have to prepare for that interview on Monday."

~FI~

Catherine had spent the best part of the day planning for this evening. She stepped out of work mode the minute she left the office on Friday afternoon, but it always took a few hours to just relax and remind herself that weekends were for fun. One on one, she could handle, but group settings put her on edge. A consequence of being *Specky Four-Eyes* at school. Subsequent laser treatment had put that option for name-calling to bed once and for all, but she had never forgotten it. The way they would surround her and taunt her. She shivered just thinking about it.

As she grew and developed her own sense of self-worth, she also became more confident. She could turn on the charm just as easily as she could turn on the ice queen. With Brooke, she hadn't felt on edge for a moment. In fact, that night had been the most comfortable Catherine had ever felt with another person.

She hadn't spotted the brunette yet, and Brooke took the opportunity to observe her. Catherine had her hair down this time. A slight curl meant that the light bounced off and made it appear as though it were dancing. She must have felt eyes on her because she turned slightly and glanced right at Brooke, her lips curving into a smile instantly.

Catherine felt her insides flip at the sight of Brooke as she made the universal signal of pretending to hold a drink, while tilting her hand and mouthing, *"Do you want a drink?"*

Even from across the room, Brooke could not ignore how captivating the blonde was as she nodded. With Brooke busy at the bar, Catherine quickly checked her make-up, running her little finger around the corners of her mouth to remove lipstick residue. Why was she so nervous? Good nervous, of course. She felt giddy and thrilled. Could Brooke be the one? There hadn't been anyone serious since Penny. She forced that thought from her mind. The last thing she needed now was an image of Penny as she packed her desk and left the office, smirking that she had won some kind of battle Catherine had never wanted to wage.

She watched as Brooke made her way over with drinks in hand, dodging between revellers and people dancing. At one point someone almost knocked her over, but she kept her balance, laughing it off as the man apologised for his exuberance.

"Hey." Brooke grinned again, placing Catherine's drink down in front of her. "You look...amazing." Brooke's dark eyes wandered the expanse of skin on display before settling on sparkling hazel eyes. Catherine had gone rather risqué in her choice of outfit for the night. She was 42 years old, but that didn't mean she had to dress like her mother did at that age, and if she was honest, she had plans for staying out all night. So, the burgundy camisole with thin straps that made it obvious she wasn't wearing a bra felt the most natural choice. Noticing Brooke's subtle glance at her chest only boosted her confidence in pulling it off.

Catherine's head tilted while she considered the compliment. "Thank you. You look rather dashing yourself."

"I thought I should make an effort." Brooke took a seat next to her. Thighs touched as she leaned in and placed a chaste kiss against Catherine's cheek.

"Oh, are we not a little further along than that?" Confidently Catherine teased, her palm reaching up to caress a lightly tanned cheek as she brought their lips together for an easygoing kiss. Despite the music and noise surrounding them, Brooke heard quite clearly the soft sigh emitted by Catherine, and it moved the butterflies in her stomach into another tumble of arousal.

The kiss broke naturally, both women smiling into the last mutual caress of lips, but they didn't move apart. "*That* was a much nicer greeting."

"You're right. I didn't want to take liberties and assume..."

Catherine's palm slid effortlessly into Brooke's lap, finding her hand and interlocking their fingers. "You can take liberties with me anytime." She smirked and raised a brow playfully. Lips met again, a scorching kiss this time, one that built with quiet passion and threatened to cause embarrassment in public. "In fact, later, I am counting on it."

The night was fun. Kissing interspersed with dancing, more kissing, and drinking. There was laughter, teasing, a whole heap of flirting, and Catherine was enthralled. The club was packed. The night for many still had several hours of dancing ahead, but Catherine was done with it. She had other plans for the night ahead, if Brooke was up for it. "Let's get out of here," she said against Brooke's ear.

The younger woman nodded and let herself be led by the hand as Catherine squeezed them through the throng and out onto the street.

The night air was definitely changing from autumn to winter. You could smell it in the air, the way winter begins to lay its cold blanket down. The warm glow of the alcohol soon wore off and

Catherine shivered. She had chosen to wear a flimsy coat that went with her outfit rather than avoid the potential hyperthermia on offer. Brooke shrugged her jacket off and hung it around her shoulders, pulling her into a tight hug in order to warm her.

"Take me home," the blonde whispered against her mouth, smiling into the kiss that followed.

"Alright."

~FI~

Brooke unlocked the door, holding it open as Catherine slipped through. She smiled as she passed into the hallway. The small flat was everything Catherine assumed it would be: homely and warm, without being overly personal. She wandered into the living room and picked up a photo frame: Brooke in full uniform. While she entertained herself, Brooke entered the small kitchen off to the side. Opening the fridge door, she grabbed two bottles from the shelf and used the bottle opener to flick the caps off. She glanced around quickly, thankful that Robin hadn't left any mess before she went over to Jas's place.

She took a swig from one bottle as she strolled back out and into the lounge, almost spraying the beer out of her mouth when she came face to face with Catherine.

In the centre of the room, in the middle of a pile of discarded clothes, Catherine stood in just her underwear and heels. Unashamed and unabashed, she strode purposefully towards Brooke. She took both bottles from her, placing one down on the table before taking a swig from the one Brooke had been drinking from. Then she placed that one down too, still smirking, as she leaned in and kissed the corner of Brooke's mouth.

"I guess I got a little impatient."

Brooke took a small step back, holding her at arm's length as she took in the shape of her.

Catherine worked out and looked after herself, that much was clear. Years of wearing heels had created perfectly toned calves. She wasn't skinny or overly toned like women on TV that Brooke sometimes crushed on. No, Catherine was a normal, beautiful and confident woman.

"So I see." Brooke grinned and reached for her. Her fingers grazing skin gently.

"You look a little overdressed. I think we should remedy that, don't you?" There was that sexy smile again. Catherine oozed confidence, and that alone was enough to turn Brooke on.

She made no effort to stop the deft fingers that loosened the buttons of her shirt and then pushed the material from her shoulders. Catherine silently appraised her bare torso. They kissed again, this time skin to skin, breast to breast. The room felt suddenly hot. She took Catherine's hand and this time, she led the way back out into the hall, the two of them giggling and kissing their way along the hallway until Brooke swung the door to her bedroom open.

Pliable lips pushed and pulled against one another as Catherine pulled her eagerly towards the bed. Fingertips gently explored soft naked flesh as gentle gasps and moans filled the air. Brooke threaded her fingers into Catherine's hair and tugged her closer just as Catherine palmed Brooke's cheeks gently.

Breaking the kiss, Catherine panted, "Still overdressed." The statement was playful and she stepped away to watch, her chest heaving as she caught her breath and waited.

Wasting no time, Brooke unbuttoned her jeans, eyes fixed on Catherine the entire time as she quickly shrugged the material to the floor, kicking one leg off and then the other. Her body was now a lot softer than it had been six months ago when army PTs had had her at the peak of physical fitness, but she didn't dislike the changes. She was still toned and healthy.

Lascivious eyes darkened as Catherine tilted her head, lips parted slightly. She ran her tongue over her lips and whispered, "Stunning."

Casually, Brooke slid her underwear down and stood back up proudly, a silent suggestion that Catherine do the same. Which she did, slowly; teasingly.

It had been so long since Brooke had been naked with another woman, not counting her colleagues in shared shower blocks and changing rooms. She didn't do this kind of thing often. But there was something different about Catherine, something attractive to her that hadn't been present in many of the other women she had dated. Those women had gone home alone at the end of the night.

Opening the bottom drawer in her bedside cabinet, she drew Catherine's attention to the black leather harness.

"Maybe later, right now though." She grabbed hold of Brooke and pushed her back onto the bed, "Right now, all I want is you."

Brooke scrabbled up the bed, pulling Catherine with her and into her arms as they flopped down together in a heap of tangled limbs. "I can live with that." She grinned and let her fingers wind into Catherine's hair, tugging her closer. Lips demanded attention, pressed together and pliable.

They rolled, together as one, with Brooke coming out on top. She rose up on her palms, and Catherine took a moment to admire the well-defined biceps. "I don't usually do this."

A candid moment that Catherine hadn't expected. "No?"

Brooke shook her head, her fringe falling forward and masking her eyes. Catherine reached up to push the hair out of the way and studied her. She felt special, honoured even, that Brooke had wanted her.

Those dark eyes that seemed to penetrate right through her were smiling at her, egging her on. Holding those eyes captive with her own, she moved her arm between them, letting her fingers dance lightly down Brooke's torso until she found her. Her fingers danced through the contours of her, finding her wet and wanting.

Brooke's eyes closed at the sensation, filling her lungs with air and expelling it slowly in one long, controlled breath. "Look at me," Catherine said in a quiet whisper. She hadn't expected this intensity between them. Every featherlight touch felt like granite pressing down on her skin, imprinting itself indelibly upon her skin, in her heart maybe.

They moved together as one, hips rising and falling, meeting each other before backing off and beginning the chase again.

She felt Brooke's hot breath against her cheek – short, erratic bursts of air between gasps. Her eyes were wide, pupils dilating as she bit down on her lip, unable to stop the soft moans of approval from leaving her mouth.

She was fascinating, and Catherine watched every imperceptible movement of her features, felt each rigid motion her body made as every muscle she had tensed and prepared for that sweet release. And then, just as her biceps began to tremble and Catherine worried if she had the vigour to hold on, Brooke tossed her head back like a glorious victor, her pelvis pressing down, jerking, shuddering against Catherine's hand until finally, she collapsed from the exertion.

Brooke giggled, enjoying the tender touch of her lover's fingers stroking lightly down her back.

"Fuck, just..." She was breathing fast. "Gimme a minute and..."

Chapter Four

Her body ached from the hours of lovemaking she and Brooke had undertaken. Catherine struggled to remember a night as hot and sexy as last night had been. It hadn't happened in a long time, if ever. Why hadn't she dated a younger woman before? She chuckled to herself.

Straddling Brooke's thighs half the night as she had ridden her toy, enjoying orgasm after orgasm, was certainly the cause of the delicious ache in her muscles. Just thinking about it re-awoke her arousal, nostrils flaring and thighs squeezing shut.

She stretched slowly and pushed herself up against her young lover. Her skin was soft and warm. She let her pelvis thrust gently against Brooke's buttocks. They were firm and taut, now harness-free. She let her hand smooth across the pert cheek, giving it a little squeeze. She groaned. God, when had she become so wanton?

Lying there, this close to someone again, Catherine wondered if she dared to consider it. There had been flings, dates and even a friend with benefits, but nobody special since Penny.

And it wasn't that she didn't want a long-term lover, because she did, but the idea of it and the reality of it were two very different things. Things she wasn't very good at. Penny had made sure she knew that.

At work, Catherine was known for being a no-nonsense, tough-talking, hard-arsed, first-class bitch. She was well aware of the names she garnered by those who worked with and for her, but she didn't care, not anymore. She had made a conscious decision the day she resigned from Modas, an enormous lesson learned.

That was work, where she held a responsible position and expected a competent work force to pull their weight for the company.

But away from the office, she was a different person. She was warm and appreciative, amusing in her own way. Not quite so confident – sometimes she still struggled with the nuances of a relationship – but love was not something she was incapable of. Trust issues were her main problem; she knew that and worked to avoid them once she was in a relationship. The problem was that she didn't often allow herself to develop a relationship with someone.

She had spent far too much time in her 42 years trying to adapt to other people and fit them into her life. Now that she had closed herself off to the idea of anyone permanent, she had found life much more interesting and a lot easier. She reminded herself just how awful it was when she had to finally admit it wasn't working. She tried, she really did, but life wasn't so simple for her. It always ended badly.

She had to admit though, not for a long time had anyone attracted her the way that Brooke had, not this quickly anyway. The younger woman was attentive and made her feel incredibly sexy, but it was more than that; she seemed genuinely interested in what Catherine had to say. She was fun and intelligent. Sometimes Catherine could barely understand the things women on the prowl talked about these days, but with Brooke, it all just seemed so natural. Maybe, she thought, maybe this woman could be different.

She fidgeted a little and snuggled in some more. *Why worry about it now*, she thought to herself, *just enjoy it while it lasts.*

~FI~

Another surprise was the lack of urgency to leave once Brooke woke. In fact, Catherine had been easily persuaded into another round of lovemaking. And then there was the shared shower that had been a surprise Catherine had not experienced before, but goodness did she want to do it again. Every morning should start like this one.

Usually, Catherine would wake before her chosen lover and quietly dress before sneaking out and heading home without all the awkward pretence of wanting to see them again. Then she would shower and go about her day with a quiet smile on her face. She checked her watch: almost 11 a.m. There would be no sneaking today.

"Would you like to get some brunch?" Brooke asked. Her hair, still damp, had gone all tousled. Catherine liked the look, a lot. She felt that tell-tale sign of arousal tug at her lower stomach once again and almost groaned out loud at her own neediness. Which was completely unwarranted considering what this woman had already given her in respect of carnal pleasure.

"No, thank you, Brooke, I really should be going. I have a lunch date with an old friend." She noted the disappointment register on Brooke's face. "I'm sorry, maybe we can have dinner sometime next week?" She stroked a palm across Brooke's cheek before buttoning her jeans. "I'll call you, okay?"

Brooke nodded. "Sure." She reminded herself that she needed to collect Robin from Jasmine's anyway.

Catherine smiled and leant in. "One more kiss to last till the next?" she whispered against smiling lips. And then she was gone, leaving Brooke with bed sheets to change and a sister to retrieve.

Chapter Five

"So, tell me all about it," Robin said, grinning widely at Brooke. They sat together on the top deck right at the front of the bus. It was raining outside, and droplets dripped down the windscreen slowly on the outside as the inside steamed up. "Is she still classy or did you ruin her?"

Brooke's eyes widened. "Where the hell did you learn that?"

"What?" She shrugged nonchalantly and giggled. "Come on, did she stay the night?"

Brooke knew her cheeks burning magenta were probably the giveaway. She ran her hand through her hair and smiled coyly. "She might have."

"I knew it!" Robin shouted. "You look too happy for this early on a Sunday." They sat quietly, both grinning to themselves as the bus reached its next stop. People moved about. Those who needed to get off were replaced by new passengers. One older lady got up and changed seats. "Miles asked me to the Christmas dance. I think I'm gonna say yes."

Brooke looked across at her. "That's not for weeks."

Robin grinned, "I know, eager!"

"So, Miles huh?"

Now it was Robin's turn to blush. "Yeah, he's cute. I mean for a *boy*."

Brooke rummaged in her pocket and pulled out a packet of gum. She took two from the packet and popped them into her mouth before offering one to Robin. She shook her head.

"So, I need a new dress...I'll help pay for it."

"Oh, and how you gonna do that then?" Brooke laughed.

"Well, I figured I'm 15 now, so..." She looked at Brooke all wide-eyed and innocent. "I can get a job."

"We already talked about that. You need to concentrate on your studies. This year is..."

"I know, I will, but Jasmine said they need seasonal workers through November and December in her dad's shop. Mr Khan said I can work Saturdays and he will pay me £5 an hour." She had it all worked out, and Brooke was a little impressed, but still, it wasn't the plan. Getting a job now was essential.

"I know it all sounds great, but its hard work, Binnie."

Robin pushed her hair back behind her ear. "I know, but only for 6 weekends. I'd earn £240 and that would buy my dress, and the rest you can have to put towards the trip." She grinned again and Brooke realised in that moment just how much older she looked.

"I tell ya what, let's see if I get this job or not." Robin sighed and pulled her bag closer to her chest.

The bus stopped again. More people got off than got on this time. The windows were still steamed up, and Robin drew a smiley face in it. "So, what's her name?"

"Huh?"

"Classy? I assume you do know her name?" Robin smirked.

"Of course I know her name," Brooke scoffed. She could feel her sister's eyes on her and buckled. "Catherine, her name is Catherine."

"Nice, what does Catherine look like? Is she hot?"

Brooke's head whipped around just as an image of Catherine, head thrown back in ecstasy, popped into her mind. "I think she is," she admitted. Robin continued to stare, one brow raised. "She's a little taller than me in her heels and she has long honey blonde hair and these greeny-brown eyes that are just..."

"And?"

"And what?"

"Do you like her?"

"When did you get so nosey?" Brooke deflected.

Robin was having none of it. "You *lurve* her," she joked and ruffled Brooke's shorter hair.

"Get off," she laughed. "I like her. It's the first time since Gabby that I've felt that connection with someone."

"Gabby was a dick," Robin stated with a sneer.

Brooke turned to face her, "You didn't even meet her."

"Didn't need to. She dumped you, therefore she is a dick."

Brooke considered chastising her for her language, but, "Yeah, she was a dick." They both laughed and high fived.

"So, you're gonna see her again, right?" It came as a question, but was meant as a statement. "I'll get out of your hair anytime you wanna bring her over, okay?"

"You don't have to do that."

Robin rested her hand on top of Brooke's. "B, you need to have a life too. It's not all about me. Just cos Dad's gone...I know you made promises to him, but we're in this together, right?"

Brooke nodded. "Yeah, Sis. Together," she said clasping her hand and squeezing gently.

~FI~

Catherine was running late, and she really hated to be late, but then, she really hated leaving Brooke too. She'd grabbed a cab from the first taxi number logged in her phone and had made it home with barely enough time to get changed. She supposed that she could have just met Ronnie as she was, but arriving in yesterday's clothing and doing the walk of shame was not something Catherine Blake ever planned to do. Especially when meeting Ronnie; the woman would rib her for months.

Luckily, she had found a parking space reasonably quickly when a blue Ford pulled out of a space just yards from the restaurant. She nabbed it, easily parking in the small space with the help of these new-fangled sensors this car had.

Entering Banjo's, she scoured the room and noted Ronnie sitting towards the back at a table for two. She had her nose in her phone and didn't look at all bothered to have been kept waiting. As though sensing that she was being watched, Ronnie looked up and ran a hand through her short, dark tresses. She waved, and there was a sparkle in her eyes that matched the smile on her face as Catherine made her way between tables.

"Hey, what time do you call this?" she laughed, exaggeratedly pointing to her wrist, where she wasn't wearing a watch. Her Scots brogue was still evident even after 25 years down south.

"I am so sorry, I got...held up."

Ronnie's brow raised immediately. "Oh, held up?" A knowing smirk followed. "So, I take it the date went well then."

There was no way that Catherine could deny otherwise. "Yes, she's...I believe I am smitten." She laughed at herself.

Ronnie sat back and appraised her. "Well, well... Catherine Blake, back in the game." Her smile was genuine. "So, you're seeing her again?"

Catherine nodded. "I would like that very much, yes. Did you order yet?" She took her reading glasses from her bag and picked up the menu.

"No, I waited for you," Ronnie answered, picking up her menu too. "You know, for a while there, I really thought you were going to stubbornly persist in this life of perpetual singledom."

Catherine shrugged. "I was always open to the idea of meeting somebody, I just...you know what it was like with Penny," she stated as she read through the options. "I think I'll have the pork."

"Good choice, I was looking at that...but then I remembered that it's a wee piggy, so I'll have the vegetable curry."

Chapter Six

With Robin locked away inside her room finishing the homework she had, Brooke was at a loss with what to do with herself. There was only so much housework anyone could do before the term "OCD" came into play.

Picking up her phone, she swiped through the apps and found a game to play. Word searches were at least keeping her brain motivated and in some form of working order. She was just inputting a new guess when a text popped up.

Catherine: I just wanted to say that last night, and this morning, were something I very much enjoyed. Cx

Brooke swung her legs down from the sofa and sat up straight, almost as if Catherine had entered the room. She was about to reply and then thought better of it. "Yes, I liked it too" wasn't quite the response this required.

Brooke: Hey, it's been a long time since I have spent any time with someone and enjoyed it as much. I look forward to seeing you again, soon? Bxx

Several minutes passed, minutes in which Brooke had convinced herself she had said too much, looked too needy, read the entire situation wrong. In the end she placed the phone under a cushion and refused to look at it for all of a minute before she picked it up again and checked for a new message. When it finally did beep, she held her breath, closed her eyes, and prayed that it was from Catherine and wasn't telling her to get lost.

Catherine: This might be totally ridiculous and maybe you're already busy, but I wondered, it's only 4 p.m., and I

can't stay out late because I have a very busy day ahead of me tomorrow, but how would you feel about going for dinner or a drink, now obviously? Cxx

Re-reading the text twice, Brooke couldn't hide the grin on her face. It was perfect. She was perfect.

Brooke: I'd love to, I just need to get changed. Shall I meet you somewhere? xx

She threw the phone down on the couch and all but ran into the hallway, knocking loudly on Robin's door. "Binnie?"

"What?" came the teenager's frustrated voice.

Brooke opened the door, and Robin swung around in her seat to face her. She had books all over her desk and bits of crumpled-up paper and banana skins decomposing around the bin. "Are you ever going to clean this room?"

Robin ignored her and stared blankly.

"Anyway, I am going out for a bit, will you be okay?"

Robin gave her best *are you kidding me* look. "Where are you going?" The grin that lit up Brooke's face gave Robin the answer. "Oh, Catherine?" she laughed. "Yeah, go. I'm just going to be in here all night anyway. I can get dinner. We do have food, right?"

Brooke nodded, laughing at her. "Yes, there is food. I think there is even some biscuits in the top cupboard."

Robin blushed and glanced guiltily towards the wrapper in the bin. "Uh, not anymore."

~FI~

Brooke swapped out her jogging pants and hoodie for blue jeans and a shirt. She looked smart and casual, perfect for an impromptu date with Catherine. Checking her watch, she suddenly panicked when she realised that she hadn't checked her phone for Catherine's reply. She almost tripped over her own feet in the rush to get it.

Catherine: Why don't I pick you up in 30 mins? We could go for a drive down to Brighton, it's not that far. X

The message had come in 17 minutes previously. "Shit." She quickly replied back.

Brooke: Sorry, I was just getting changed. Sounds like a plan! I'm ready to go so I'll see you when you get here. Xxx

With no further reply from Catherine, Brooke sat herself down on the sofa to wait. The butterflies of anticipation, however, fluttered so much that she had to get up and do something. Her reflection in the mirror gained her attention. She ran her fingers through her hair several times, pulling it in one direction and then the other until she was satisfied that she looked okay. It was growing out and was in that in-between stage of just hanging loose on top. The back and sides she had kept quite short with a trip to the barber. Once the top grew out, then she would let the rest start to grow with it. She hadn't had long hair since she was a kid, and it intrigued her a little to see what she would look like with it now.

A new text message pulled her from her thoughts.

Catherine: I'm outside, xx

"Robin? I'm off, I'll see you later. Don't stay up late," she was saying as she pulled on her bomber jacket at the door.

"Okay, have fun." Brooke was sure that she detected a giggle in Robin's voice.

"I mean it, don't stay up late. You've got school in the morning."

"Yes, Mum!"

Chapter Seven

A black SUV flashed its lights at her. Crossing the street towards it, she could see Catherine inside, waving and smiling at her.

"Nice car," Brooke said as she climbed in and leant across to place a kiss on Catherine's smiling lips.

"It gets me from A to B," she replied. "I didn't interrupt your evening plans, did I?"

Brooke laughed. An evening sitting by herself watching TV was the worst plan that she could think of. "No, I actually didn't have any plans."

Catherine pulled the car out into the road. "I haven't done this in a while," she admitted as she concentrated on joining the traffic at the end of Brooke's street.

"Me either, I haven't been to Brighton in years."

Catherine chuckled. "Actually, I meant this...dating someone. I've...it's been a while since I've found anyone that I'd be remotely interested in spending time with." She actually surprised herself with how candid she was being with Brooke. It was something else that she hadn't been like with anyone other than Ronnie lately.

"If it makes you feel any better, I'm not exactly inundated with offers...I kind of withdrew from dating lately, too many other things going on," Brooke replied with equal honestly. "And I've always been of the opinion that you don't need to look for these things; the right person will find you." She grinned, unashamedly staring at Catherine as she drove.

"Did you have a nice lunch with your friend?" Brooke asked, wanting to know all there was to know about this woman.

Catherine glanced across at her. "I did. We don't get to catch up too often, but I'm trying to be a better friend." She laughed at herself. "Did you do anything interesting?" she wanted to add, *without me.*

"I spent the afternoon with my sister."

The roads were reasonably clear of traffic and the journey was smooth. A local radio station played in the background, something poppy and upbeat but turned down too low to be intrusive on their conversation.

As the motorway came to an end and the road weaved slowly into Brighton, Brooke realised just how easy the drive had been. Even in the silences, it hadn't felt awkward. Catherine hummed away quietly at times, while Brooke threw out little comments about the journey, places of interest, or stories from her own youth when her friends had just started to drive and they would all pile into cars and head down here for the evening. Of course, then she had joined the army, and all her friends had moved on.

"I found a few on social media and we've chatted a bit, but it's not the same, is it?" Brooke said, staring out of the window. It was dark already and not even 6 p.m.

"You didn't keep in touch while you were away?"

Brooke shook her head. "Nah. I wanted to, and for a while we all tried but, it's not like I could just drop everything in Kandahar and stick a selfie up on Instagram." She grinned.

"No, I suppose not." The thought suddenly struck Catherine of how much worldlier Brooke was compared to herself. She had barely left the UK – a few European beach holidays, but mainly she had stuck to climbing the ladder. "Do you miss it?"

"Being shot at?" Brooke smirked. "In a strange way I do. It was tough, don't get me wrong, you never have a good night's sleep while you're potentially in the line of fire. There was always the risk of a bomb or a rocket, so even when you thought you were safely ensconced on base, you never truly let your guard down. But, you're in it together, you and your mates. We're a team and regardless of who you are, where you come from, or what's between your legs, we had each other's backs and that's something special, ya know?"

Catherine didn't know. "I guess I am more of a loner. School wasn't much fun for me and then I went to university and it wasn't much better, though I did meet Ronnie, so it wasn't all bad." She smiled, but Brooke noted the hint of sadness there. "I don't make friends easily."

"That surprises me," Brooke said. "You have been good fun, articulate and entertaining so far. I can't see why anyone wouldn't want to spend time with you."

Catherine blushed. She was silent for a moment as she concentrated at the roundabout. With the next gap in the traffic, she pulled forward quickly and took the turn that would lead them along the seafront to where all of the pay-and-display parking spaces were. "I find myself very much at ease with you, Brooke." There was a space up ahead and she moved the car into it. Yanking the handbrake, she turned to the darker of them and leant forward. Cupping Brooke's cheek, she guided her forward. "There's something about you that I just...I can't resist." Their lips met, and when she asked for entrance, Brooke submitted in an instant. Her tongue was hot as it slid into her mouth and caressed her own. Brooke wasted no time in joining Catherine's passion. Her fingers found their way to entwine in thick hair, grasping handfuls as her breathing upped a notch and became erratic while she tried to keep breathing through her nose. Anything she could do to just keep kissing this woman, she would try. When Catherine finally pulled away, she groaned at the loss. Catherine chuckled. "If we don't stop now, then I fear we might never leave the car."

"Is that a bad thing?"

Catherine grinned. "Come on, let's have some fun."

~FI~

Fun meant heading to the pier and cashing up pound coins for 2p coins. Catherine was in her element on the tipping point games, patiently waiting for the right moment to drop her coin and watch as it rolled or dropped down onto the moving platform to line up flat and be pushed forward. Any time she knocked coins off, she would jump excitedly and cling to Brooke, grinning like a child who had just won a balloon at the fair.

Brooke preferred the driving games, but only played one as she didn't want to waste what little money she had on such frivolous activities. "I need to find a cash point," she said as Catherine dropped her last coin into the machine.

"Why?" she asked, bending slightly to watch the coin fall into the one space where it would do absolutely nothing.

"Because I've run out of cash." She laughed.

"Brooke, please, this is my treat." Catherine said, straitening up and facing her. She stood as close as she could and let her palms lay flat against Brooke's shoulders. "I asked you to join me. You can pay next time." She leant in and took Brooke's lower lip between her own, sucking gently before releasing it and smiling coyly. "Or you can pay in kind."

Brooke laughed. "I think that's a given. I just like to pay my way."

"Good, because I'd really hate to date a cheapskate." She grabbed Brooke's hand and pulled her. "Come on, I want a penguin." She laughed as they headed towards the shooting stall. "You can show me your skills."

Chapter Eight

Brooke woke up Monday morning in the best mood she had been in for weeks. Catherine had dropped her off just before midnight and she had slept like a baby. Well, she had done once she had stopped thinking about that good night kiss, the kiss that had led to a lot of over- and under-clothes fumbling. She felt like a teenager again, sitting in a car in the dark, parked along the street away from the streetlamp. When Catherine climbed over the console and sat in her lap, Brooke thought all her birthdays had come at once. When Catherine had unbuttoned her jeans and pushed Brooke's hand inside, Brooke thought all her Christmases had come at once as well.

She chuckled at the memory of Catherine pushing her out of the car and replacing her in the seat with the giant penguin Brooke had won for her.

"Robin, you up?" she called out, banging on her sister's door. "You've got 5 minutes or a bucket of cold water is coming in to say good morning," she warned playfully.

"You wouldn't dare," came the sleepy reply from behind the door.

She chuckled. No, she wouldn't dare, but only because she wouldn't be able to dry the mattress. "Wanna find out? Come on, you've got school and I need to get ready for this interview."

The door opened and a messy-haired teenager with one eye closed frowned at her. "Good luck," she said as she passed by her and shuffled into the bathroom.

"I'll do some breakfast then," Brooke shouted after her.

~FI~

Being in the army had taught her early on in life to be confident in her abilities, and she knew that this was a job she could do with her eyes closed. Pollards would be stupid to turn down someone with Brooke's experience and know-how.

She arrived early. She was perfectly presentable in clean white shirt and navy trousers, pressed impeccably, and she had not a hair out of place. Her shoes were shined so well that the sun reflected off of them as she walked.

The waiting room wasn't that large. Just enough room for a handful of chairs, a small coffee table, and a coffee machine. A man in his fifties had already taken the seat in the corner. He was obviously the next candidate, and she smiled at him as she poured a small cup of coffee. He nodded and went back to reading his paper.

The door opened and another man, this time a lot younger, maybe in his thirties, came out. His face was red, and he didn't look happy.

"What a bitch," he muttered as he left the room. Brooke and the older man raised eyebrows at each other, but before either of them could speak, his name was called.

"Good luck," Brooke said as he stood up and adjusted his tie.

"Thanks."

~FI~

His interview barely lasted ten minutes before the door opened and he two came out looking flushed. "Blimey, I've never been interrogated like that before. Good luck." He smiled, but made a hasty retreat, leaving Brooke alone in the room again. She swallowed and took a deep breath. "You can do this," she said to herself. "You have to do this, Robin is counting on you."

The door opened. "Ms Chambers?"

She stood up and tried to smile, confident in her own abilities. She followed the woman into the room. It was bright and airy; it smelt freshly painted and clean.

A lonely chair sat by itself in the centre of the room, and in front of it was a long table with three people sitting behind it, all three looking at her. Two were smiling; one looked as though she might faint.

~FI~

Catherine Blake, Head of Human Resources, was sitting right opposite her – back ramrod straight, chin up, and eyes wide. A perfect reflection of Brooke's initial reaction. Catherine, *her* Catherine, was the same woman who would decide whether or not she got this job.

How was it possible that the woman, who was cavorting naked in her bed just two nights earlier, was now the person to decide if she would be employed or not? It had to be a sign, right? It was fate, kismet! She tried not to appear overly confident, but she had this in the bag. Apart from Catherine, she really could do this job with her eyes shut. It was a walk in the park compared to the streets of Kabul. All she had to do was sit tight, think straight, and give them no option but to hire her.

They threw all of their questions at her, and she batted them back with the right answers, and enough charm and wit to definitely secure the older woman's vote.

The older guy, Paul something (she couldn't remember, as introductions were done at the same time that she was gulping in air at seeing Catherine), seemed more intent on catching her out, occasionally asking the same question but in a different way. So, she answered with the same answer, only in a different way. The small smirk on Catherine's face didn't escape her notice. She was impressed too.

Twenty minutes she had been in there when Catherine told her it was "lovely to meet you" and "we will be in touch as soon as possible."

They held eye contact for as long as was polite, but Brooke found it difficult to look away.

She left the building feeling pretty upbeat. Things seemed to be looking up, with the potential job and Catherine – well, she definitely wanted to see where they went.

The bus stop was right outside the store, and she waited in line with everyone else. She was pretty much the only one not laden down with shopping bags. Her phone buzzed inside her pocket. A text message had come through now that she had turned the phone back on. It was from Robin, wishing her all the best. She grinned and was putting the phone back into her pocket when it beeped again.

Catherine: Can we meet tonight to discuss this new development? Catherine.

Brooke grinned. Seeing Catherine tonight would just be the icing on the cake. The bus was pulling in, and everyone lurched forward in order to keep their space in the queue.

Forget it

She checked her watch. It was already 3 o'clock, just enough time to head home, grab a shower, and get changed into something more comfortable before meeting Catherine at Art for 7 p.m.

Chapter Nine

Art was beginning to feel like home, and in Brooke's mind, it was starting to feel like their bar. The place was definitely growing on Brooke as she sat at a small booth and waited. She could feel butterflies, her tummy fluttering with those telltale signs of nervous anticipation and arousal.

Checking her watch for the fourth time, she saw it had only been a minute since she had last looked. She glanced over at the door and watched. Each time the door opened and Catherine failed to enter, she found her foot started tapping. She had never been this eager to see someone previously, not even with Gabby. She closed her eyes and relaxed her shoulders. She needed to get a grip. Opening her eyes, she was pleasantly surprised to find Catherine was standing in front of her. She jumped her feet instantly, smiling as she leant in to kiss her. Catherine turned her cheek just enough that the kiss just caught the corner of her mouth. Unperturbed, Brooke sat back down, patting the seat beside her.

Catherine placed her briefcase on the bench seat opposite Brooke and slid in alongside it. Now, Brooke was intrigued. Narrowing her eyes at the other woman, she noted the look of uncertainty, and then, as though Catherine had made a decision in that moment, she looked away, swallowing hard. Brooke's earlier exuberance was now replaced with a different kind of nervousness.

Turning back, Catherine smiled briefly at the glass of wine. "Thank you," she said, taking a sip.

Brooke felt her heart beating faster in her chest. Her gut instinct was already firing early warning signals, but she wasn't quite sure why. She trusted it though; it had never let her down before.

Catherine placed the glass down gently and pushed it away with her fingertips. "Very thoughtful of you." She smiled again, but this time her eyes didn't quite smile along. "Firstly, I'd like to say that I had no idea you would be interviewing today. We don't get given names until the day we interview." When Brooke looked confused, she continued. "In case we make up a preconceived judgement about someone, I never look at the list. The candidate either is or isn't perfect for the job, so I didn't know it would be you until you walked through that door."

"Okay, it doesn't matter," Brooke offered. She reached across the table with her hand, hoping that Catherine would take it. She didn't.

"You'll be pleased to know that you got the job. Kim and Paul were very impressed – as was I," she added quickly. "Official confirmation will come in the post, but we'd like you to start as soon as possible."

"That's great, I can't wait to start." She grinned, but Catherine's face remained passive.

"Yes, and that's why I want to make it very clear that this can go no further," she said, waving her hand between them both.

Brooke felt it like a punch to the gut, or a swift kick to the solar plexus that would leave a man down, winded and vomiting. "What? Why?"

"I'm sure you can understand my dilemma. In giving you the job, I cannot then be seen to be seeing you outside of work. That would be extremely unprofessional and not to mention, unfair on yourself. People would make assumptions about how you got the job. It's also against Pollards policy for staff to fraternise," she said, clarifying her decision.

The long swallow of her lager felt like molasses pouring down her throat, smothering the emotional lump that wanted to scream out loud like a toddler in a tantrum about the unfairness of it all.

"So, I thought it only fair to do this face to face," Catherine continued. She took another sip of her drink, but it left a bitter taste in her mouth and she promptly stood up, reaching for her briefcase. Pursed lips frowned. "Monday, 9 a.m. on the dot."

When she turned to leave, Brooke reached out and gripped her wrist. "Catherine, wait."

She stopped, but didn't turn around, and Brooke released her grip. Standing quickly, she moved around and into her personal space to face her. "Surely we can work around this? I know we just met but, don't you feel it? This connection we have?" Catherine remained silent, her eyes darting around the room, looking anywhere but her. "I won't take the job. I can work anywhere." But in her heart, she knew that it wasn't an option right now. Robin needed her to be working. Her little sister needed stability and a school trip to be paid for.

"No." Catherine shook her head slowly, her teeth worrying her lower lip. "Take the job, you need it. This was just...fun." She shrugged and walked away, calling over her shoulder as she lifted her phone to her ear, "9 a.m. Ms Chambers, my office."

Slumping back into her seat, Brooke picked up her bottle to drink, but as it hit her lip she frowned and placed it back down on the table. "Fuck!"

Chapter Ten

The cold air hit Catherine's face just as the first tear slid down her cheek. Holding the phone tightly to her ear, she walked with purpose towards her car and listened as the call rang out and went to voicemail.

"Ronnie, I need...get back to me when you can."

Disconnecting the call, she put the phone into the console and wiped her face. She needed to get a grip. From the moment that Brooke stepped into the interview room, she knew this would be the outcome. No matter how much she liked her, she couldn't and wouldn't put herself through that again. She liked working at Pollards and had built a reputation based on respect and her work values. Nobody would ever have the opportunity to ruin that again. Penny had been a big lesson, one she had learnt from. It was better to nip this in the bud right now than risk it all again.

Walking into Art, she had it all planned out in her head, what she would say and how she would react. A cool, detached demeanour would work. She hadn't planned on Brooke being so distraught. She hadn't allowed herself to really believe that Brooke was seeing this as anything more than fun. That thought had made it easier to end things, but now, as she sat in her car and watched Brooke walk out of Art and away – hands tucked into the pockets of her jacket, shoulders slumped, looking lost – she felt like she had made a big mistake.

Starting the engine, she checked her mirrors and pulled out onto the street. When she drove past Brooke, it took all she had not to pull over, wind the window down, and offer her a lift. She shook her head. This was for the best; she knew that.

Her phone rang through the speaker system and nudged her from her thoughts. She pressed the button to answer the call hands-free.

"Hello."

"Hey, it's me...sounded pretty urgent so I figured I'd call right back," Ronnie said through the speakers.

"Yes, I..."

"Cat, what's wrong?!" She smiled wryly; only Ronnie got away with calling her Cat. "You wanna come over?"

"Already on my way," she replied, indicating to turn left.

~Fl~

Ronnie lived in an affluent part of town. The houses there were oversized and underpopulated in Catherine's opinion, but Ronnie hadn't cared and bought the home of her dreams regardless of Catherine's indifference to it.

They had been best friends since meeting at University all those years ago. What had started off as a brief sexual liaison had quickly turned into the best friendship either of them could have hoped for. Ronnie was probably Catherine's only real friend. She tended to keep herself guarded; walls went up around strangers. It wasn't that Catherine was unsocial, because she wasn't; she often tagged along with Ronnie and her friends to Art or other bars and events, and she joined in with conversations and looked to most people like she was having a great time, but Ronnie could tell when she was uncomfortable. It had been that way the other week when Catherine had met them in Art. Carl and John were celebrating their engagement, and Ronnie had invited Catherine and another friend, Petra, to join them for a few drinks. It had been fun, but Catherine hadn't really settled. Not until her head had been turned by the brunette across the bar.

"So, what's the drama?" Ronnie said, smiling as she held the wide door open for her best friend. The smile dropped when she realised that Catherine had been crying.

Catherine shook her head, unable to hold off the tears any longer, and fell into Ronnie's arms.

"Oh, hey come on, let's get you inside, and a wee dram I think." She guided Catherine into the familiar home and got her seated on the couch while she poured a couple of glasses of Scotch. "Here, get that down ya neck and tell me what's happened?"

Catherine was reminded of the first night they had really talked, when she had opened up about her life at school, at the hands of bullies. She was always the butt of someone else's jokes. Ronnie had been there; a boy from her village had caused her nothing but problems until she punched him square in the face. Catherine had initially been shocked, but then laughter bubbled up and broke free. From then on, they had a bond that went deeper than any friends with benefits relationship could ever have been.

Catherine downed the Scotch in one mouthful and then grimaced at the heat of it as it rushed down her throat, burning away the bile of frustration. "I ended things with Brooke," she stated, wiping her face with a tissue.

Ronnie frowned. "The hot baby dyke that just yesterday you were smitten with?"

Catherine nodded. "Can I have another?" she asked, holding the empty glass up. Ronnie raised a brow. Catherine didn't usually drink on a work night, but she stood up and brought the bottle over.

Refilling their glasses, she asked, "So, why?"

Catherine sighed, her hand running through her hair in frustration. "Because," she began, slipping her heels off and pulling her legs up under her on the couch, "she was interviewed today for a position at Pollards and I could find no reason to turn her down."

Realisation hit Ronnie in an instance. "Oh...and of course you can't possibly work with someone you're fucking." It wasn't a question; she already knew the answer.

"I...you know what Penny did." Catherine closed her eyes and tried not think back to that time.

"Yes, and I also know that Penny was a bitch and you should have dumped her long before she managed to—"

"Ruin my life? Yes, I know, and that's why I can't risk that again." She picked up the glass and this time sipped at the drink, shaking her head. "You of all people know what I was like after that."

Ronnie did indeed know what she was like after Penny and it wasn't pretty, but she also knew that Catherine had a tendency to revert back into her teenage shell the moment anyone came close to climbing those walls she had built. "Well, you could...but you won't, and that is a travesty, because you deserve to be happy, Cat. And yesterday, you were happy with her, and today you're unhappy...without her. Doesn't that say something?"

"I barely know her. It was a lot of fun, and this is for the best," Catherine insisted, trying to convince herself. Ronnie wasn't so sure. "Plus, let's face it, she's 26."

Ronnie laughed. "And so what?"

"I'm 42, how long before that becomes an issue? When her friends find out and the jokes start?"

"Oh Catherine, you know at some point you're going to have to just trust someone and grow a thicker skin. You're going to walk away from someone, the first person in a long time that has seriously turned your head, because she's younger than you?"

"And works at Pollards," Catherine added, sipping her drink some more.

"Age isn't an issue nowadays; all the kids are doing it." She laughed and poured another drink.

Catherine sighed and swallowed down the last of the Scotch. "Yes, it's all wonderful now...but what about ten years from now when she's in her sexual prime and I'm getting wrinklier by the minute?!"

The roar of laughter from her friend made her jump. "Oh my God, will you listen to yaself, Hen. You're gorgeous at 42 and you'll be just as gorgeous a decade later. Don't close yourself off to potentially the best thing that has happened to you in your entire life, just because of a whole heap of 'what ifs.'"

Chapter Eleven

Monday morning found Brooke standing outside of Pollards with twenty minutes to spare. She had spent the entire weekend trying to decide if she should come here at all, and why it was that for the first time in years she had met someone decent, someone she felt a connection with, only for nothing to come of it.

To say she felt cheated would be an understatement. Catherine had been right; she needed this job, and that was the only reason why she was standing here in the cold, weeks before Christmas. Checking her bank balance had put any thought of refusing right out of the window. One of the bonuses of this job had been that it was an immediate start, and in six months she would get a store discount card and a raise.

She blew out a frustrated breath and watched as customers flooded into Pollards. She checked her watch again and then followed them in. An older gentleman in a store uniform smiled and greeted Brooke as she wandered inside. "You look a bit lost, anything I can help you with?"

"I start working here today," she said with a half-smile. "Not sure where I am supposed to go."

He chuckled. "Well, I've seen happier people on their first day. You'll wanna head over to Customer Services, they'll sort you out. I'm Stan, by the way."

"Thanks, Stan. I guess I am a little nervous. I'll see you around," she said, waving back to him as she walked in the direction he had pointed to.

"Good morning, welcome to Pollards." Apparently, all Pollards staff were good-natured in the morning, she mused. Immaculately dressed and wearing a name tag that read Jeffrey, he stood proudly in his uniform behind the big desk that marked them apart.

"Good morning, Jeffrey. My name is Brooke Chambers. I start work today, but I'm not sure where I need to go first."

He smiled again. "Oh how wonderful, we do so love a new member to the team. I imagine heading up to HR will do the trick." He looked over her shoulder and noticed a young woman. "Amber?" he called out. The woman stopped instantly to look in the direction she heard her name called from, pulling an earbud from her left ear. Her lips curved upwards when she realised who it was. "You're heading up to HR, would you show Brooke the way, she is starting today?"

Amber lit up like a tree at Christmas. Everything about her seemed bright and sunny. Office staff clearly didn't have to wear a uniform, and she made the most of it with her big comfy yellow knit sweater and cobalt blue trouser combination. "Sure, hi Brooke. Welcome to Pollards." Her hair had, Brooke assumed, originally been one of the shades of blonde. Now it was an amalgam of pinks, purples, and reds.

Brooke tried a smile and pretty much pulled it off. She followed Amber across the shop floor and through a door out the back. Half way up the two flights of stairs, Brooke asked, "You work in HR then?"

"I do indeed. I guess you've already met Ms Frosty Knickers?" She smirked and added a wink. "At the interview?"

"Uh..." Brooke shrugged. "There were two women on the panel...so..." Brooke felt her cheeks colour, almost to the same hue as Amber's hair.

"Ah, yeah, Kim is great...she works with me in the office, we do all the day-to-day stuff. Paul is head of security, but they probably told you about that."

Brooke nodded, sure now that "Frosty Knickers" was Catherine. "Yeah, they mentioned that." Amber's heels click-clacked as they climbed the steps.

"Well, anyway I am sure you'll do fine and not need to deal with Frosty."

"Uh, why?"

Amber stopped and turned as she hit the top step. It was probably the only way the shorter woman was ever on anyone else's eye level. "The only time we deal with anyone up here is when they start working here, stop working here, or get into trouble." She eyed Brooke up and down before adding, "You don't look like trouble to me."

Brooke laughed nervously. "Well, let's hope so."

Pollards was an old-fashioned department store that kept everything they did in house. "This is payroll, you'll wanna know where they are. Trust me, if you do overtime, keep track." Amber leant in. "Sandra and Alex are forever cocking that up."

It was a maze of corridors and doors that led to various offices and departments. As they passed each one, Amber would point it out and give a brief description of what they did and who worked there, imparting nuggets of gossip and information that Brooke assumed was part of working life here at the store.

Forget it

The HR department was made up of three inter-connecting rooms. There was one main office where three desks filled the space as well as a bank of filing cabinets along one wall. Shelving filled with files lined another wall. A photocopier and printer took up the largest space against yet another wall. There was a small window that overlooked the parking area outside, but at least it was natural light, and in the distance, you could see as far as the city.

Two doors led off from the right. The first was a meeting room. Through the portal window in the door, Brooke could see a long table that could comfortably sit maybe 10 people, and there was a large whiteboard with the evidence of the last meeting still scrawled across it. A larger window looked out across the glass roof of the main part of the store in a different direction to the main office window. The last door was exactly the same as all of the others, except for the name plate, a black rectangle of plastic with the words "Ms Blake - Head of Human Resources" stamped into it. It was clearly Catherine's office.

Brooke felt her insides roil at the thought of seeing Catherine again. She checked her watch (five minutes to the hour) and ran a hand through her short hair, grateful for the extra time she had spent this morning getting ready. At least she felt good about herself, presentable and ready for whatever this job – and Catherine – threw at her. Or so she thought.

"Good luck," Amber whispered as Brooke readied herself to enter Catherine's office. Optimistically, she hoped that given a few days to think, when things had settled down a bit, maybe they could pick up where they left off.

Her knuckles tapped against the door, butterflies building as she waited. It felt like an age before she heard the quiet, *"Come in."* Exhaling, she pressed the handle down and slowly opened the door.

She should have prepared herself better, should have stopped herself from thinking anything more about Catherine Blake, because seeing her sitting at her desk staring up at her as though she were just another person was like a slap in the face. But then she reminded herself that that was all she was. The thought hurt.

"Take a seat," Catherine said, her voice void of any emotion. She turned back to her computer screen and finished typing something with barely a glance at Brooke. When she was finished, she turned back and looked up, finally giving Brooke her attention. "Thank you for being so prompt, if it's one thing I cannot abide it's tardiness." She removed her glasses, folding the arms and placing them gently down on her desk.

"I was in the army," Brooke reminded her as she sat down. She sat up straight, hands resting easily in her lap. She looked confident and composed to anyone looking in, but inside she was battling the urge not to start throwing up all the questions she had at her.

"Of course." The image of Brooke's photograph in her uniform flashed across Catherine's memory, but it was banished in seconds. "So, this week you will spend the majority of your time here in the office. Towards the end of the week you'll probably start shadowing with Mr Stone in store."

Catherine Blake at the office was not the same Catherine that was occasionally found at a bar, and definitely not the same Catherine that let loose between the sheets, Brooke considered. The woman sitting opposite her certainly looked like Catherine. Her voice was similar too, but the sultry sexiness from before was replaced with a stern, matter-of-fact coolness that permeated the room like a nasty bout of flu.

"So, as you will find, Pollards is a company that takes its health and safety extremely seriously," she continued as Brooke zoned in and out from her own thoughts, her mind trying to comprehend who this woman was and failing completely. An enigma, she decided.

"You'll be expected to read and sign the various SOPs, of course..."

"Sorry, what?"

"Standard Operating Procedures." Catherine's head tilted to the left. "Ms Chambers, I do hope that your attention to detail will be far better once on the shop floor?"

Brooke felt a tight smile purse her lips at the admonishment. She bit back the thoughts that ran through her head. *Uh huh, you seemed to like my attention to detail.* Instead, she went with the politer, "Yes, sorry Catherine..."

"It's Ms Blake," she warned. "And you will do well to remember that."

Brooke stiffened at the second reprimand. How could this woman be so different, and why? It didn't make any sense, and that was the biggest frustration to Brooke. She wanted to add her own rebuke, starting with why the hell was she being such a bitch? But she bit her tongue.

"I'll put you with Amber for the rest of the day. She will go through them with you. Tomorrow you will report to Paul Stone, he is your team leader and he will get you kitted out in uniform, and then you can return to Amber until you're up to speed with things." She looked up to make sure that Brooke was paying attention. "Then it's up to you."

"Up to me?"

"Yes, whether you stay at Pollards or decide the job isn't for you."

Brooke scoffed. "The *job* will be fine." She stood up. "is there anything else? Or should I just run along?"

Catherine sat back in her chair and observed her fleetingly. "There is no need for that attitude."

There was a need for the attitude, but getting sacked on her first day wasn't something she wanted on her CV. "I am sorry. I just don't—"

Catherine breathed deeply. "If this is going to be too difficult for you, Ms Chambers..."

Brooke threw up her palms. "No, it's fine. I guess it's just a little disconcerting to have you behave like we never even met before when in fact, I've seen you naked and made you come, several times." She lowered her voice, but the intent was there.

Catherine smarted, and looked as though she were about to reply when she thought better of it. Instead, she picked up a file and opened it. Without looking up again, she said, "Amber will give you everything you need."

The sound of the door clicking closed drew Catherine's attention to the emptiness of the room; it felt suffocating. She placed her pen down and sat back, sighing deeply. This was not going to be as easy as she had convinced herself it would be.

Brooke Chambers was not just another employee.

Chapter Twelve

Sliding her key into the lock, Brooke could already hear the loud rap music blasting out from the stereo in Robin's room. She entered her home unheard and wandered down the hallway. At least Robin had made it home safely from school. Checking her watch, it was just after 7 p.m. Her little sister had been home for at least 3 hours. She sighed and prepared herself for the mess that would greet her.

"Hey, I'm home," she called out, kicking her shoes off and tossing her jacket over a chair. Tiredness was creeping up on her as the minutes ticked by. All she wanted to do was shower, crawl into bed, and forget about Catherine Blake.

The room was surprisingly tidy. Robin's schoolbag lay haphazardly on the sofa, but at least it was closed and not spewing books all over the place like usual. She picked it up and moved it to the floor next to Jasmine's. "Robin!" she shouted. The door to the youngster's bedroom opened and Jasmine Khan's head poked out with a big cheesy grin plastered to her face.

"Oh hey, Brooke!" Her head popped back into the room. The music stopped abruptly and Jasmine reappeared, followed by Robin as both girls exited the bedroom, giggling and jostling with each other playfully.

"Hey, Sis. How did it go?" Robin flopped down on the couch, pulling Jas with her. The pair of them continued to giggle as they landed in a heap.

"It was okay, I guess."

Robin frowned. Brooke didn't sound happy at all. She also didn't look as though she wanted to talk about it, so she let it go. "That's good, I cooked dinner." Robin announced. Jumping to her feet again, she pulled Jasmine up with her. "Oh, and Jas is staying over. That okay?" The pair had wanted to do something special for Brooke's first day at work. Mrs Khan had agreed and allowed Jas to stay over. Even though it was a school night, she knew her daughter and Robin were good influences on each other.

"Sure, what did you cook?" She wasn't that surprised; Robin had been taking a big interest in cooking and the kitchen lately. She liked watching those cookery programs on the TV and if the interest in art, history, and archaeology tailed off, then Brooke expected a career in cookery to take its place.

"Spag Bol, but I put some spinach in it so it's more like a Florentine," she called over her shoulder knowingly. "Wanna beer?"

"Nah, I'm good. How long have I got?"

Jas poked her head out of the kitchen. "Ten minutes, but we can hold off the spaghetti."

"Okay, can I get time to grab a quick shower?"

"Whatever ya want," Jas called back before heading back into the kitchen. "You think she looked a little sad?" She watched as Robin opened a cupboard and measured out the right amount of spaghetti for the three of them.

"Yeah, I thought that. Maybe she just had a busy day, or the new girlfriend hasn't called."

"I guess." Jas considered the other possibility. Brooke was nice. There was no way the girlfriend wouldn't have called, surely.

"Tired, probably." She reached into the drawer and pulled out cutlery to lay the table, setting up three placings. "What did she say about working for my dad?"

"I'm working on her. At the moment she's all *no way Robin, you need to study*...but, I have a few more tricks up my sleeve."

"It will be so much fun. Dad is barely there and as long as we get the jobs done, he doesn't mind if we mess about. Unless it's in front of the customers. Then it's a big no no." She grinned and pulled three plates from the cupboard.

Robin stirred the pot, lifted the spoon to taste, and shook her head. "Needs more salt," she said as much to herself than to Jasmine. "If she has this Catherine to keep her busy, then she will want me out of her hair."

"True, and we do not want to be hanging around here if they're gonna be kissy-face all the time."

Robin grimaced. "Ugh, I so do not need to witness that." Both girls fell about laughing. "Anyway, I have plans to be kissy-facing myself, with Miles."

Chapter Thirteen

The alarm went off at exactly 6:39 a.m. Brooke groaned and threw the cover off. It was getting colder in the mornings now, and she shivered a little as her bare feet hit the laminate flooring. A stark reminder that she needed to buy a rug.

She had set the alarm twenty-one minutes early, knowing full well if she didn't then two teenagers would hog the bathroom for the best part of an hour and she would be late to work on her second day. Plus, 21 was a good number.

As the hot water washed over her, she considered just climbing back under the covers. She could stay here and avoid Catherine Blake altogether, but the other part of her had the "fuck it" attitude of going in to work and showing Catherine Blake just what she was missing. Her "fuck it" attitude always won out.

The one positive thing about a cold room was that she dried off and dressed in record time. Mission accomplished, she headed to the kitchen to make some tea and to toast a couple of slices of bread. Heavy breakfasts had never been her thing. Unless she was being frog-marched on a 15-mile hike with a 30-pound backpack on her back – then she would load up on carbs galore – but deskbound at Pollards, she figured the toast would suffice. Plus, she could always grab something at the canteen.

The girls shuffled past her in the hallway, Jas heading for the bathroom, while Robin pushed into the kitchen first.

"Morning," Brooke said.

"Hmm," mumbled her sister, eyes half-closed against the bright fluorescent lighting.

Forget it

Brooke chuckled and hit the button on the kettle. "Want some tea?"

"Please," Robin managed as she pulled the fridge door open and found the bowls of overnight oats they had made the night before. She left them on the table and returned to the fridge to get some orange juice. "Brooke? You okay?" she asked, her head inside the cold box.

Putting down the tea caddy, Brooke turned her way. "Yeah, why?"

Finally, Robin found the OJ and put the carton on the table beside the oats. "Dunno, you just look a little unhappy."

Her toast popped and she made a grab for it, juggling the hot slice onto the plate. "I'm fine, just a long day. Lots of stuff to remember." She smiled it off, but Robin wasn't convinced.

"You said the one thing we always had, other than each other, was honesty."

Brooke nodded, caught in her own web. "You're right." She took a bite out of her toast and swallowed down a swig of tea before she had finished chewing. "I guess I am just a little upset that I won't be seeing Catherine anymore."

Robin stopped pouring the juice, her eyes widening at this news. "But I thought..."

"Yeah, me too, but turns out she's my boss, kind of."

"Holy fuck!" Robin exclaimed before clamping a hand over her mouth. "Sorry, but...how?"

Brooke shrugged and grabbed her jacket from the back of the chair. "Shit happens, I guess. Look, I'll be fine, don't worry about me." Opening her wallet, she pulled a five-pound note from it and held it out to Robin. "I'll be alright. Get something for lunch and do not buy chips."

The youngster took it and tossed it on the table. "It's fine, I made sandwiches."

~FI~

At least Amber had been fun. Spending the morning reading through more SOPs and getting the lowdown on more of the goings-on at Pollards was somewhat entertaining and helped to take her mind off of the icy blonde in the next room.

Even line manager Paul Stone seemed pleasant enough now he wasn't interviewing her. He ran a tight ship, but she was used to that. Taking orders was fine by her.

He kitted her out in a full uniform, which wasn't that bad as uniforms went. It consisted of a black shirt with epaulettes and breast pockets. It had the Pollards logo sewn into the left pocket flap, but it was barely visible. With the shirt went black slacks with a workable utility belt and black steel toe-capped boots that made her army boots look totally inferior. Thankfully, there was a bomber jacket too. The word "security" was printed across the back in bold white lettering, and it had silver hi-vis stripping, but it was warm. It could have been a lot worse. The entire ensemble was topped off with a peaked cap that was probably a little over the top. In truth, she looked pretty smart. She knew how to pull off a uniform, though the clip-on tie was pretty naff, but she could suck it up.

Getting back to the office from her foray downstairs, Brooke walked in and almost bumped straight into Catherine. She stood just inside of the doorway, speaking to Amber.

"Sorry," Brooke mumbled, taking a step back. For a moment, Catherine just stared at her before finally stepping aside to let her pass. "Thanks."

Catherine's gaze followed her in before she abruptly turned back to Amber to finish her instructions. "I found Adams next to Atkinson, and Jones was completely misfiled under N. Go through them all and please, this time make sure that alphabetical indeed means a, b, c."

"Yes, Miss Blake. I don't know how that could have happened."

"I imagine it's down to a lack of focus Amber, too much chit chat and not enough organising." She hugged the files she held to her chest. "I will be gone for the rest of the afternoon, please ensure that Ms Chambers is not interrupted with office gossip."

Brooke's gaze followed her as she left. "Is that what she's always like?"

Kim sighed. "Pretty much. She's still an improvement on Malcolm. Cup of tea?"

Brooke nodded. "I'll make it while you two interrupt me with all the gossip." She grinned.

Chapter Fourteen

Amber had the tea brewing when Brooke entered the office the following morning. Her back to the door, she heard rather than saw the new security guard enter. "Tea is made and I even brought bickies!" she said, smiling as she turned around holding up a packet of chocolate digestives. "Wow, you scrub up okay in that," she said, indicating the uniform.

"Yeah, figured that I might as well wear it in." Brooke grinned and reached out for the mug of hot tea. She stood there warming her hands around it while waiting for Amber to finish her own drink. "So, we the first ones in?"

Amber nodded. "Yep, though Frosty Knickers won't be long. She is always here eight thirty on the dot," she replied, glancing up at the large white clock on the wall. It read 8.28 a.m. Brooke watched as Amber set up her desk again, making space for Brooke to read through the rest of her paperwork. Brooke smiled in thanks and placed the mug down on the desktop to shrug off her jacket; it was suddenly stifling in the office. She hung it on the back of her chair, just in time to see the door opening. Glancing up, she saw that the clock did indeed read 8.30 a.m.

"Morning, Ms Blake," Amber said as chirpily as she could manage. Her blonde boss inclined her head to her assistant before bright eyes swept around to lay upon Brooke. Catherine felt her chest tighten as she took in the sight before her, eyes drawn to the black leather utility belt around Brooke's waist, which was reminiscent of something quite similar that she had worn in a totally different situation between them. She snapped her eyes back to Amber. Safer territory.

"Miss Simmons. Ms Chambers," she acknowledged before slipping into her office, the door closed firmly behind her.

With the coast now clear, Amber giggled. "Told you, you look good in that uniform, did you see the way she looked at you?" she whispered. "I always thought she was your average, straight, no nonsense, ice queen; maybe all she needs is a hot young security guard to thaw her out a bit. Go on, take one for the team," she pleaded.

Brooke felt her cheeks burn, picturing Catherine naked in her bed. "Pretty sure that I am the last person Ms Blake is interested in," she said. Plonking down and picking up the first form, she began reading, aware that Amber was staring at her. She gave in and finally looked up. "What?"

Amber raised an eye, pursing her lips. "Are you always so self-deprecating?"

Brooke shrugged and found a piece of lint stuck to her jumper to fixate on. Amber walked over to the filing cabinet and flicked through a few files, her eyes still on Brooke.

"I've never seen Ms Blake blush before," Kim piped up as she too took in the scene being played out.

"Do you think she has a boyfriend?" Amber queried, picking out a file and moving it to its correct position. "I can't imagine it, she's so..." She stopped what she was doing and searched for the word.

"Private?" Brooke suggested, feeling the need to try and protect Catherine still.

"Well, yeah. But if she's this cold at work, she must be an iceberg in bed."

"Maybe she's right," Brooke huffed. "We should be concentrating on work?" Catherine Blake was anything but cold in the bedroom. It would have been easier if she had been. That would have made sense to Brooke now as she tried to fathom it out. An unconnected, uninterested Catherine Blake in bed would be so much easier to get over.

"Of course, she's right, one can never accuse Ms Blake of being wrong, just a little chilly and reserved." Amber shrugged. "Anyway, doesn't matter to any of us what she's like outside of work, does it?"

Silence filled the space as everyone returned back to their tasks.

Only Brooke struggled to concentrate.

Chapter Fifteen

Pollards was a large store. In addition to top quality food items, they sold everything from clothing to electrical goods and even had a small cafeteria. It was nicer than the tiny canteen for staff that was upstairs, hidden away from public view. There were no rules on staff having to eat there as opposed to the nicer café, but many of the shop floor staff preferred it as they could escape the public for a little while.

Amber, however, liked to get out from behind the desk and immerse herself in humanity. So, Brooke joined her. She figured it was as good a place as any to start getting a feel for the place. They joined the short queue and made their orders. Brooke chose a bean burger and chips, only feeling slightly guilty that she had ordered the very thing she told Robin not to eat.

There were several empty tables, and Amber led the way towards one that looked over a balustrade, right across the store. She nabbed a chip off of Brooke's plate.

"Hey, get ya own." She laughed, looking down at the quinoa salad Amber was having. It didn't look like much, and she wondered how anyone survived on such measly rations.

"They always taste better when they are someone else's." Amber grinned in return.

"Yeah, well that might be a lot safer when the someone else isn't someone trained to kill," Brooke deadpanned back in response.

Amber sat back in her chair and studied Brooke. "Trained to kill, huh? You don't look too scary to me."

Brooke smirked and chomped down on a chip. "Well, looks can be deceiving."

As they chatted amiably about less important matters, Brooke caught the flick of blonde hair in her periphery. Still listening to Amber, she turned her head slightly and found her eyes locked with those of Catherine Blake. The older woman looked away instantly and back to her newspaper, but Brooke kept staring. Catherine's face was almost hidden now by the paper. She looked good though, and that thought alone sent Brooke's stomach into somersaults. Everything about Catherine screamed leave me alone: the way she sat, legs crossed and turned away from everyone else, elbows pulled into her side. She looked compact and confined.

Brooke just couldn't fathom out how the Catherine she had met at Art and invited to her bed was the same Catherine sitting by herself across the room acting all cool as ice. She turned back to Amber and smiled at what she was saying. Her ex-boyfriend was sniffing around, and she was enjoying the attention but had no intention of getting back with him. "Once a cheat, always a cheat, that's what my mum says, and she's right."

"I guess so. Trust is a very important factor in any relationship, isn't it?" Brooke replied, glancing back towards Catherine.

"Indeed, and anyway I've got my eye on someone else."

Brooke raised an eyebrow in interest. "Oh, who?"

Amber blushed a little. "He works in the clothing department." She looked over the balcony and pointed. "Over there, with the short dark hair, Brian."

"Brian?"

"Don't laugh, he can't help what his parents called him." She giggled. "He's cute *and* he is nice, which is more than can be said for a lot of people around here." She glanced quickly towards Catherine now too.

Brooke's brow furrowed as she considered this new information. "So, it's not frowned upon to be seeing someone you work with in store?"

Amber shook her head. "Nope, nothing in the SOPs bans fraternisation. All it says is that in the event of two people being romantically linked, they should not work in the same department."

Remembering Catherine's words, she asked, "Wait, so, if someone was head of a department, could they date anyone else, there must be rules in place for that, surely?"

Again, Amber shook her head. "No, so long as they do not work together. So, for instance, old Frosty Knickers wouldn't be allowed to date me or Kim, because we work directly under her. In that instance, I or Kim." She scrunched up her face at the idea. "Let's say Kim, Kim would have to be moved to a different department. Payroll maybe or, anyway it doesn't matter, cos Old Frosty Knickers and Kim? That's hilarious."

Brooke tried to smile at the joke, but failed miserably. Instead, she picked up her drink and hid her disappointment behind the white china. Catherine had lied to her.

~FI~

They were barely back into the office when Catherine's door opened. "Ms Chambers, may I see you, please?" She didn't wait for an answer before closing the door behind her.

Brooke and Amber shared a look, raised eyebrows on both faces. "If you're not out in 5, I'll rescue you." Amber giggled in hushed tones.

Standing, Brooke straightened out her clothing and walked towards the office, her mind awash with ideas. Some of them were not appropriate for an office. She smirked as she entered the room that housed Catherine Blake for eight to ten hours a day. Maybe Catherine had finally come to her senses and realised that there could be something more between them.

Catherine sat behind her desk. Her hair was now held in place by a rather complicated-looking hairclip. Being this close to her again brought a shiver down Brooke's spine. Her perfume permeated the air and once again, images that Brooke didn't want right now reared their head.

She waited, thumb tucked into her belt as she leant all of her weight to one side and tried to appear casual and not bothered. Catherine was reading something and hadn't looked up, nor did it appear that she would, so Brooke almost jumped when she spoke. "Please, take a seat," she said, her voice not quite so confident either.

Brooke did as she was asked and got herself comfortable in the chair, her line of vision now right on Catherine's face. She studied her for a moment. Her glasses magnified the tiny lines around her eyes just a little. She had done a good job covering them with make-up, not that they bothered Brooke. She liked a woman with experience of life. She looked a little tired to Brooke, dark circles under her eyes again covered with make-up. Brooke wondered what kept her up at night. Or who?

Catherine looked up, doing a quick sweep of the woman opposite before her eyes settled rather firmly on Brooke's face.

"I think this afternoon you can shadow Mr Stone," she announced rather abruptly.

"Okay."

Brooke waited for further information, instructions or just a hello, how have you been, which would have been nice. But nothing further came. She shifted in her seat, the movement gaining Catherine's attention.

She barely looked up from her paperwork again. "You may go."

Brooke half stood. "Is this how it's going to be?"

Catherine raised her head and squinted at her. "I'm sorry, what?"

Brooke sat back down again and looked at her. "I get it, I'm a big girl. I've had knockbacks before; honest ones, mind you." Catherine frowned and looked at her as though she had spoken a foreign language. "You didn't have to make up the whole 'fraternising at work' thing just to dump me. And this whole ice queen routine," she waved her hand around, "it's not necessary."

Catherine sat back, she wasn't shocked that Brooke would speak so honestly, or call her out on the little white lie she had told, and she probably did deserve an apology for that. "You're right, I shouldn't have lied and for that, I am sorry."

Brooke nodded, appreciating the apology. "So, I think it would be prudent to meet outside of work and discuss this so we can...put it to bed, so to speak."

Catherine was already shaking her head. "No, I don't think... that wouldn't be wise. We had a...flirtation, it was fun at the time and now it's over."

"A flirtation, that's an interesting word choice." Brooke smiled sadly as she stared into those eyes that couldn't hide their attraction. "So, you didn't...there isn't a connection for you? It was just sex?"

The army taught Brooke many things, and reading people better was one of them. She could tell now that Catherine was thinking about something, a memory. From the look on her face, it was a sad memory. "Yes, it was." She sat up straighter in her chair, as though that in itself would deflect Brooke's unbelieving gaze.

"I don't believe you," Brooke replied. People lied all the time; Brooke knew that. Some lies mattered and others, not so much, but this one, this lie that Catherine was prepared to tell, it mattered. "When you're walking the streets of Kabul and you see someone, you need to rely on your instincts. It's a gut thing. To be able to look at someone and know when they're being truthful? It's a matter of life or death, quite literally."

She spoke softly as Catherine listened, but said nothing. But then she laughed, catching Catherine by surprise, "I'm sorry," Brooke chuckled wryly. "It's just that this is farcical. I like you, you like me, and here we are doing nothing about it." Still, Catherine remained silent, but her breathing grew more ragged.

"Okay, I'm going to go downstairs and find Paul. I'll get out of your hair for a bit, give you some breathing space to think this through." She stood and walked to the door, and then she turned back.

"Life is too short, Catherine."

Chapter Sixteen

Catherine's office suddenly felt claustrophobic. The minute the door closed behind Brooke, she let go of the breath she was holding and gasped. She got up and moved quickly to the window, flinging it open and allowing the cold air inside. Her skin burned, with —embarrassment? Arousal? She didn't know, but the heat she felt whenever Brooke Chambers was around was almost unbearable.

She sucked in calming breaths. In through the nose, out through the mouth, until she felt back in control. It was ridiculous; she was a grown woman, not a teenager with rampant hormones. Shivering now, she closed the window and sat back down in her chair. How on earth had she underestimated the effect Brooke in a uniform would have on her?

It had been the right thing to do, sending her downstairs for the afternoon. Tomorrow, Catherine would instruct Amber to hurry Brooke through the last SOPs and then she would be Paul's problem. So long as Catherine avoided the store as much as possible, then she wouldn't keep bumping into Brooke and she could get over this, what was it? Infatuation? Fantasy? Whatever, one more day and she could get on with life as she had planned it and forget all about Brooke Chambers.

~FI~

Rush hour traffic was never fun, but especially not when Brooke had a plan and she needed Robin's help. Finally, the bus ploughed through and up the hill to where Brooke could jump off and run the rest of the way. As she rounded the gate and headed up the pathway that led to her flat, she passed a boy with his hood up. Tall with a cropped afro and beautiful caramel skin, he was handsome, but maybe a little shy as he dropped his head and kept walking. He had gained her attention enough, however, for her to take another look over her shoulder. He didn't live here. Shrugging him off, she climbed the stairs two at a time till she reached the second floor and got her key out ready.

She flew through the door at such a speed she almost knocked Robin over as she stood behind it, taking off her own jacket.

"Oh, hey Brooke. You're uh...early."

Brooke came to a halt. "Where have you been?"

Wide-eyed innocence stared back at her.

"Robin, we talked about this, unless you tell me where you're going, then I assume you came straight home from school." She took her own jacket off and hung it next to Robin's

"Oh Brooke, I was just outside," she huffed, turning to walk away.

"Outside?

Robin recognised the questioning tone. Brooke was anything but stupid. "Uh, yes."

Brooke's eyes squinted at her, reading the situation. Realisation sunk in. "The boy in the hood..." she said, as much to herself as Robin.

Her sister's face reddened in an instant. "What?"

"Outside, when I was coming in, a boy your age passed me looking a little shifty."

Robin giggled. "Miles isn't shifty."

"Oh, Miles?" She playfully pushed Robin down the hall to the kitchen. "Your boyfriend?"

"Just a friend."

Twice today Brooke had found herself looking into the eyes of a female and seeing the lie that lived there. "Just a friend, huh?" She smiled over at her sister. "A cute friend?"

"Shut up." She laughed and playfully slapped Brooke's arm. "What's for tea?"

Brooke let her off the hook. It was good to see her sister happier. Since losing their dad, it had been tough for Robin. Those first few months while Brooke organised leaving the forces had meant Robin was shipped around between family and friends. Compassionate leave had only lasted for the first two weeks. Then Robin was packed off to their dad's sister in Cardiff for two months until she kicked up enough stink about missing school and her friends. Yasmeen and Dev had been life savers when they offered to take Robin until Brooke was sorted. Now, six months on, Robin was smiling again.

"Let's get a take-away," Brooke offered.

"Yeah? Can we afford it?"

Brooke shook her head, grinning. "What did I tell you, let me worry about money, okay?"

"Okay. Fish and chips then?" Robin said, ready to go get her coat on.

"Yeah, sure, but uh...can you do me a favour first?"

"Of course, what is it?"

Brooke grinned, an idea from earlier poking at her. "I need a photo of me in my uniform."

~Fl~

As glasses of chardonnay went, this one was going fast. It was the second already from this bottle. Catherine Blake took another large gulp and sank down further into the bubbles, letting the heat of the water in the bath soothe her. She had been wound like a clock for days, and she knew why. It was bloody obvious why; Brooke Chambers was why.

She took another gulp and swallowed it down with a satisfying smack of her lips. It was just her luck to meet someone who would ignite her nether regions along with her heart again, only for them to turn out to be the one person she couldn't possibly date. What had she done to anger the gods that they would play such a cruel trick on her? And it irritated her that Brooke was right; it was farcical, and she did like her, but that didn't mean it could be anything more than it was, did it? Because it couldn't; anything more was just out of the question.

Her day had been long, boring, and exhausting, with dull meetings and paperwork that she couldn't concentrate on. She had gotten barely anything done. Thoughts of Brooke Chambers constantly invaded her mind. That was why she had had to remove her from the office in the afternoon. It was bad enough knowing she existed, that she was within the building, but when she was sitting outside of her office door Catherine could hear the low murmur of conversation, the occasional laughter and movement. All of it reminded her of their date – or was it dates? – not that it mattered now.

Closing her eyes, she took deep breaths. A self-help book long ago from Ronnie had helped her to learn how to calm down. She wished Ronnie was here now. Well, not literally; their days of sharing baths and beds were long over. That didn't mean, however, that she couldn't call her up.

Shaking the water from her hand, she reached out and grabbed her mobile from the loo seat (an impromptu table anytime she had a bath). A tiny green light pulsed, alerting her to a message.

As soon as she had swiped a finger across the screen to wake it, she regretted it. Brooke Chambers' name lit up. She slammed the phone back down and groaned.

"Why?" she said to nobody but herself. Curiosity got the better of her though, and she found the phone with a fingertip search while refusing to look. She kept her eyes closed, right up until the phone was in front of her face, and then she swiped the screen and pressed against Brooke's name – and almost dropped the phone into the water.

The picture image that filled the screen was the last thing Catherine needed tonight. Her arousal levels were already going haywire since the night she had spent with Brooke. Just 48 hours of enjoying the feeling of being interested in somebody again, and then it was all wiped away in an instant when the fourth candidate of the day had strolled in and sat down in front of her.

She glanced at the photo again. God, she looked good in that uniform. The tie was missing and the top two, or was it three, buttons were undone. The buckle on the belt hung open, as did the button to her trousers. Brooke's stance was casual, leaning easily to one side with a hand in her pocket and a tilt of her head, the cap placed on top of her head. She zoomed in and out of the photo, examining every pixel. Everything about it said *come and get me*. Including the short message attached.

Catherine could only imagine how sexy she must have been in a military uniform. Her body was a traitor. Her skin flushed and no matter how much she tried to ignore that tummy-flipping sensation that sent a pulse straight down to her clit, it was impossible. She needed to touch herself. If she was ever to ease this feeling of need and want, then she would have to give in. Her thighs squeezed tightly together, the water sloshing at the movement.

"Dammit," she said aloud, her voice echoing slightly in the small room. Her hand moved instantaneously to the right spot. Pressing down to relieve the constant throb, she was determined not to give in. She would not get off over a photograph of Brooke Chambers standing there with her left hand tucked inside her pocket, all casual and carefree. But she didn't need a photograph; the images of their night together flashed constantly in her mind.

Her fingers though, had a life of their own, moving in tight circles.

"No." She shook her head and yanked her hand from the water. Pulling the plug, she climbed out, straight into the shower. Cold water instantly brought about the end to this bout of arousal.

"Damn you, Brooke!" she cried out as she slumped against the cold tiles and slid to the floor, hot tears streaking her cheeks.

Chapter Seventeen

Catherine Blake arrived on time as usual the following morning and found an empty office. Amber's computer was on, so her colleague was at least here and wouldn't be in need of a reprimand.

A stack of paperwork sat neatly on top of the desk where Brooke had been stationed these past couple of days too, so there was life somewhere. She breathed a sigh of relief that Brooke wasn't there, smiling at her and looking all sexy and...she shook those images from her thoughts and moved quickly to her own office. Closing the door with a thud, she leant against it and breathed out slowly. She had made it. Now, she could ensconce herself inside for the entire morning and then after lunch, send Brooke out with Paul for the rest of the day. Nodding to herself, she shrugged off her warm woollen coat and hung it on the hook. Its magenta colour stood out against the indifferent magnolia walls.

It was a lot colder now on the way to and from work. November had definitely brought with it a winter chill. At lunchtime, she considered that she might head down into the store and purchase a new hat and scarf, and maybe one of those hot drink travel mugs. Then she could enjoy her morning tea in the car on the drive in, rather than swallowing it down as quickly as possible in order to beat the traffic.

That was when she noticed it: right there in the middle of her desk, a cardboard take-away cup and a paper bag from the cafeteria downstairs. She opened the door and took another look around the office. Both Amber and Brooke had similar cups on their desks. Still no sign of either of them.

Catherine closed the door again and considered the offering. It had to be Brooke. Not once had Amber, or Kim for that matter, ever brought her a hot drink from the café. They had made cups of tea in the office and usually offered to make one for Catherine if she happened to be there when the kettle was boiling, but she had always declined, and they had stopped asking. So, it had to be from Brooke. Kind, considerate, and generous Brooke.

She reached out a tentative hand and let the back of her fingers touch the container. Still warm. It was a nice gesture, but not one that she could entertain. Accepting the gift would encourage Brooke to continue. She didn't wish to be wooed, not here at the office anyway. Curiosity got the better of her though, and she opened the bag gingerly. Pain au Chocolat. Her stomach traitorously rumbled, but she scrunched the bag closed, picked it up along with the beverage, and took them both into the outer office. She placed them down on the desk and turned to return to her office when she heard Amber giggling at something Kim had said to Brooke down the hallway.

They all stopped in the doorway as each pair of eyes moved from Catherine, to the desk, and back to Catherine again.

"I uh…" Catherine swallowed, her mouth suddenly dry. "Thank you, but I have had breakfast." She turned on her heels and promptly escaped the scrutiny.

Amber and Kim both smiled sadly. "Well, I hate to say I told ya so, but…" Kim said. When Brooke had arrived earlier carrying a cardboard cup carrier with three teas and a coffee, along with a bag of pastries, she had said right away that getting one for

Catherine was pointless; she had never accepted an offer of a drink previously. But Brooke had been insistent that it would be rude to buy for them and leave Catherine out. She left out the part of Operation Thaw.

She had spent the previous evening filling Robin in on what had happened with Catherine, how obvious it was that there was an attraction between them and how she wanted to try to convince her that she was worth a shot. Between them they came up with their plan, starting with Brooke doing nice things, little things that were not too overt.

Brooke shrugged off the embarrassed flush. "Oh well." She picked up the bag, took out the pastry, shoved half of it into her mouth and chewed. "No point in wasting a good pastry," she said, struggling to swallow it down with the lump that appeared in her throat.

"It was a nice gesture, but now you know. Catherine Blake isn't interested in us. She is the ice queen, always has been."

Brooke nodded. She understood how they could only perceive Catherine in that way, but she knew differently. Underneath this hostile exterior was a hot, molten and sexy woman, hiding from them all.

The soft click of Catherine's door shutting was barely audible.

~FI~

Catherine didn't leave her office the entire morning. When Amber, Kim, and Brooke returned from lunch, there was a note on the desk.

Ms Chambers,

I have arranged for you to spend the rest of the day with Mr Stone on the shop floor.

I expect by lunchtime tomorrow for you to have completed all necessary paperwork and be up to date with all computer-based theory work.

You will then report directly to Mr Stone and no longer be required in HR.

C Blake

"Well, it was fun while it lasted," Amber said, reading the note over her shoulder. "We can still get lunch together though, right."

Brooke smiled at her new friend. "Yeah, when I'm not on silly shift patterns." She grabbed her coat and headed for the door, with one final glance towards Catherine's office door. "See you in the morning."

Chapter Eighteen

The following morning when Catherine came into her office, she found flowers. No note. Just a bunch of beautiful yellow roses. Initially, she smiled; it had been a long time since anyone had brought her flowers or even attempted to romance her. But then reality kicked in and she sighed. There had been no sign of Brooke anywhere, but she knew they had to be from her.

"Amber," she called out into the outer office.

The young woman scurried in. "Yes, Ms Blake?" She too smiled when she noticed the bouquet. "Oh, those are beautiful. Shall I find a vase?"

"No, you shall not find a vase. Please take these and do as you want with them." She held her breath and waited for Amber to remove them from her desk. "And where is Ms Chambers? Is she late?"

Amber lifted the bouquet and brought it to her nose, inhaling gently.

Exhaling slowly, Catherine wondered for a brief moment if maybe she had been hasty with the flowers. Maybe they weren't from Brooke after all.

"No, Ms Blake. She uh...last night after you went home, she came back and finished off...she's downstairs with Paul, I mean, Mr Stone."

"Fine, then back to work." She was hopeful that maybe now, the gifts would stop, but something unfamiliar nagged at her: disappointment.

~FI~

Paul Stone was a middle-aged man, balding, already with a slight paunch. He liked a quiet life; he liked the horse racing and a home-cooked meal. He didn't go to the pub that often because he "couldn't be doing with the kids that filled the place up and vomited everywhere."

What he did like however, was a "shipshape store and no little fecker's getting their grubby little thieving hands on anything, not on his watch."

Brooke liked him. He was fair and honest and he didn't take any prisoners. If she fucked up, she'd know about it, but equally, when she got it right, he would be just as full of praise. For the first couple of afternoons, she had just shadowed him around the store. He introduced her to other staff members and a few regular customers that knew him by name.

"So, you know the layout now, right? Exit points and high-theft items. If they look suspicious, it's cos they are suspicious. Don't be afraid to be obvious, make them feel intimidated. We want them to know that Pollards doesn't like them," he said as they walked back through consumables towards the seasonal specials. "Christmas brings them all out, so peepers open at all times."

Brooke nodded and adjusted her cap, moving the peak down and into a more comfortable position. "Yes, will do."

"Brilliant, now I am going to pair you up with Potter. He started a couple of months ago, so you should have plenty in common and he can show you the ropes."

~FI~

She found Robin and Jas sitting side by side on the sofa when she got home that evening. Both were already in PJs and eating cornflakes from mismatched bowls. Brooke sat down opposite in the armchair and waited for the spewing of words that would come now she was home.

"So," Robin began, "Jas is staying over and I've roped her into Operation Thaw. I had to explain that as she thought I said Thor and was expecting a hunk of Swedish love to be waiting for her when we got home," she rattled off at speed and with barely a breath between sentences. In fact, had she written it down, there would probably have been the grammar police knocking at the door for a lack of commas and an overabundance of exclamation marks.

"Right," Brooke replied, a little unsure whether this was a good idea still.

"Oh, and there are only crackers and that hummus stuff you like for dinner, so we went with this. How was your day?"

Brooke kicked off her shoes. "It was okay."

"Did you see her?" Jas asked. Placing her bowl down on the table, she crossed her legs underneath her and leaned forward with elbows on her knees, she rested her chin in her hands to listen intently.

"Nah, I got in early, left the flowers, and went downstairs."

"But she got the flowers, right?" Robin asked.

Brooke nodded slowly, her lips pressed together in a thin line that brought frown lines to her forehead. "Yeah, and then she gave them to Amber and told her to get rid."

"Dammit, she's a tough cookie, anyone bought me flowers I'd be weak at the knees." Jas laughed.

"Only if it was Simeon," Robin teased, nudging her friend with her shoulder. She stopped laughing when she caught the look of sadness on Brooke's features. "Sorry, Brooke."

"Yeah, sorry," Jas followed.

Brooke sighed. "It's fine. I guess she just isn't interested."

"Oh no, no way are we giving up this easily, Sis," Robin announced. She banged her bowl down on the table and stood up. "There is no way that the Catherine you describe is this cold-hearted cow, there has to be more to it. She liked you enough to sleep with you, and up until you turned up at that interview, she was all for seeing you again." Jas nodded furiously in agreement with her bestie. "So, all we need to do is up the stakes, make her see that you are the best option for her."

"Yeah, she has to come in to work tomorrow and find the one thing on her desk that she can't ignore," Jas agreed.

Brooke shook her head.

"I dunno guys, it feels a bit weird...she's just not that into me."

Chapter Nineteen

The staff parking bays were almost already full when Catherine pulled into the car park. She had to drive up two different lanes before she found a space big enough to park her SUV. She still wasn't really sure why she had bought the thing. It was much bigger than her last car, and it wasn't like she was an off-roader who spent most of her down time squelching through mud. But she had to admit, it was comfortable.

The car was now nice and warm inside, and she sat there and enjoyed it a moment longer before needing to step out into the cold morning air. This morning she had needed to spend five minutes scraping off the frost and ice from the overnight chill, and now she felt a different kind of shiver go down her spine as she contemplated going in to work. A Brooke Chambers kind of shiver.

It was Friday; just eight more hours until a Brooke-free weekend. She had plans for a spa retreat, somewhere she could go and lose herself in pampering and self-indulgence and not think about Brooke Chambers. At least Brooke was out of the office now, which meant there would be no more surprise gifts left on her desk. It would be fine, she assured herself as she opened the door and climbed out.

Passing through the store's front entrance doors, she was greeted by Stan. He had worked here almost as long as the store had been open. Catherine knew this because she made it her business to know. When she had arrived at Pollards just under two years ago, she had gone over every personnel file. The previous incumbent of the position she held, Malcolm Turnbell, had been, according to Kim, a miserable sod who took little to no interest in the staff. Catherine never wanted to be a Malcolm Turnbell and yet, that was how her staff viewed her. She shuddered at the memory of Amber's words. *Catherine Blake isn't interested in us, she's the Ice Queen.*

"Good morning, Stan." She smiled, waving her hand at him.

He grinned back. "Oh good morning, Ms Blake. Your niece is waiting for you, I said they should sit in the cafeteria."

Catherine frowned. "My niece?"

"Oh yes, lovely young girl. She said it had been a while since she had visited her favourite aunt."

"Right, I should probably go and find her then." This was an intriguing moment. Catherine didn't have a niece, or a nephew; in fact, she didn't have siblings at all.

~FI~

Potter was already in the staff lounge waiting for Brooke. He had two cups of tea made and was preparing his kit for the day. He was overly fastidious, which Brooke found interesting, bearing in mind her background in the armed forces and the requirement to shine every button and boot.

In the few hours she had spent with Potter (first name unknown), she had learned that he probably had superhero syndrome. He had failed twice at the police fitness test due to his inability to run very fast or for long periods of time. He then tried for the Fire Brigade and was turned down because he had failed the police fitness test, so apparently there was no way he would get through the brigades testing. So, he had given up and took the next best thing that provided a uniform and some power: security guard.

"Morning Chambers," he said brightly, holding out the mug for her.

"It's Brooke," she said, for the fourth time since meeting him.

"I know, but 'Chambers and Potter' sounds so much more...professional," he replied, adjusting his cap and wiping imaginary dirt from his name plate, which read "S Potter." She couldn't help but think of him in an anorak, out in the rain on a weekend, watching trains. "Spotter" echoed loudly in her head and made her grin. "Shall we begin our rounds then?"

~FI~

The cafeteria was filled with people all trying to get their breakfast, staff finishing the night shift and those just starting, as well as customers enjoying a treat. Catherine quickly swept her eyes around for Brooke and was relieved not to find her here. Early morning shoppers dropped in for coffee before doing their weekly shop. Friends bumped into one another and chin-wagged over a pot of tea and cakes. She had no idea what her *niece* looked like, so she looked for the most out of place person she could find. There were two that fit the bill of young girls, and they both sat together looking at their mobile phones.

One was Asian, the other white; both had long black hair pulled into tidy ponytails. But only one looked somewhat familiar.

She strode confidently across the floor until she stood right next to their table and waited. The Indian girl looked up first. A quick nudge of her elbow got her friends attention.

"Which one of you would be my niece?" she asked, one brow raised as both girls blushed.

"Uh, that would be me." A hand nervously raised as Robin Chambers admitted her guilt. "I uh, was hoping I...*we* could have a word with you."

Catherine checked her watch; she was going to be late. For the first time during her employment, she would be late to her office. Not that it mattered; she was in charge. She could pretty much work the hours she wanted to, take time off if she wanted to, but she didn't. Instead, she liked to be here on time, setting an example.

She sat down in the seat on the opposite side of the booth, a little intrigued as well as annoyed. "You have one minute," she said sternly, unwinding her scarf and unbuttoning her coat.

Both girls looked at one another, a seriousness settling between them. Whatever they had planned was now in play, and the gravity of it had brought with it a nervous stutter. Jas nodded at Robin, who turned back to face Catherine. "You're just like she said you were." When Catherine looked confused, she continued. "I mean, she said you were gorgeous, and she was absolutely right. Do you buy your make-up here?" Robin was rambling, and Jas thumped her thigh with her fist. "Sorry, I uh...okay, see the thing is, my sister, she really likes you. Like, she's head over heels and she, well she's trying really hard so you can see she is worth taking a chance on, and..."

"Wait." Catherine raised a hand; the likeness was obvious now. "You're Brooke's sister?"

Robin grinned, pleased that Catherine at least knew that Brooke existed. "Yes, Robin Chambers, and this is my best friend, Jas, Jasmine Khan."

Catherine nodded slowly with a tight smile, but felt her spine stiffen, anxious to move away from this situation.

"The thing is, Brooke, she's a really great person, if you'd just give her a chance, go out with her again and maybe..."

Catherine raised a hand once more. "Thank you, Robin. I am sure that Brooke is quite capable of...I will speak to Brooke later, and I am sure we can find a solution to this problem. It's very sweet of you to care so much about your sister and you should definitely keep doing that, but really this is an adult situation, and one only Brooke and myself can navigate." She checked her watch once more. "I really need to get to my office. I assume you can find your way out and," she noted the school uniform, "get to school okay?"

She stood and waited for them to grab their things, then she walked them to the cafeteria exit and watched them walk off, jostling and smiling at one another. Teenage exuberance.

~FI~

Amber stared at the clock. Something was very wrong. 8:34 a.m. and Catherine hadn't arrived. She looked over at Kim, whose forehead had wrinkled in confusion too.

"Do you think she is ill?" Amber said, still looking at the clock.

"Maybe, has she been ill before?"

Amber shook her head. "Not while I've been here."

Before Kim could reply, the door flew open and Catherine thundered into the room, slamming the door behind her. "Get Brooke Chambers up here now!" she demanded before storming into her office, almost knocking the door off its hinges as she went.

Silently, Amber stared at Kim.

"Now," came the demand again through the closed door, making both women jump.

Amber grabbed the phone and called down to Customer Services.

"Hi, yes, it's Amber in HR. Can you put a call out for Brooke Chambers to come to the office immediately." She listened to the person on the other end of the line. "Yes, thank you, right away."

Chapter Twenty

Catherine paced the room, back and forth. Furious was an understatement; she had never been so livid, or embarrassed. Actually, that was a lie. She had felt exactly like this two years ago, and she hated it. It brought back way too many memories and was the very reason she had called a halt to all of this in the first place.

The light knocking on her door brought her thoughts to a direct halt too. Rather than answering like she normally would, with a polite "come in," she yanked the handle. Brooke stood on the other side looking all sexy and unconcerned, and that just pissed Catherine off some more.

"You wanted to see me?" She had that cocky grin on her face that under any other circumstance Catherine might find attractive, but not now that she knew the reason for it was humiliating her.

Catherine didn't reply; instead she stood aside and watched as Brooke passed her acting all oblivious. When she was inside, Catherine poked her head out. "You can take a break, both of you," she said to Amber and then looked towards Kim. She didn't wait for their reply either before she slammed the door shut.

Catherine stood by the door, hands on hips. Brooke watched her trying to control her temper with deep breathing, her eyes closed. Something, or someone, had upset her, that was for sure. Brooke frowned, contemplating what this had to do with her and why she had been instructed to come to the office.

Catherine took one last deep breath; she would not allow this to go on any longer. "I have *never* in my *entire* career had to deal with the utter...I can't even find the words," she began, pushing a hand through her hair. Glaring at Brooke, she stalked around her desk, anger not just written, but scrawled all over her face. "How dare you?" she finally accused.

Brooke shook her head. "I'm sorry, I don't..." She didn't get a chance to finish before Catherine's rant continued.

"It was one thing bringing me cups of tea and cakes, I can even forgive the flowers, but I will not tolerate sending a child to guilt me into dating you!" she exclaimed angrily.

Brooke stared at her blankly. *What was she talking about?* "I'm not sure I..."

"Enough. This is tantamount to..." She was going to accuse stalking, but didn't get the chance before she herself was cut off by a now very confused Brooke.

"What? I don't understand." Her own anger began to spike. "What exactly am I being accused of?"

Catherine scoffed. "Please, don't try and deny it now. Because of you, I was late. Because of this little charade, I had to sit and listen as my *potential* love life was mapped out for me by a teenager and her friend."

Brooke's mouth went dry at the realisation of Operation Thaw. Her cheeks began to burn and her stomach churned all at once. This must be what being inside a tumble dryer felt like. She thought she might actually faint. *No, they wouldn't have? Surely not,* she thought to herself. *Robin isn't that stupid, is she?* "Catherine, you have to under—"

"It's *Ms Blake,*" she hissed. "It's Ms Blake and you will cease with this...this campaign right now." The flat of her hands landed on the desk, fingers splayed as she leant forwards, spelling it out for Brooke, "There is *nothing* between us and there will be *nothing* between us. What happened needs to be forgotten, do I make myself clear? *Forget it,* Brooke." She cursed herself for the name slip. "From now on there will be no more gifts, no more photos sent to my private number, in fact you will delete that number right now." She watched as Brooke pulled her phone from her pocket and scrolled through her contacts list. Mortified, she deleted the number and then held it up as proof. "I will not have you, *or anyone*, humiliate me at work like this again. Am I clear?" Brooke nodded. "You can consider this a verbal warning. Now, get back downstairs and do your job."

"But..."

"*I said, forget it,*" she hissed.

Brooke nodded. Tears threatened to escape, but she blinked them back and turned abruptly to leave. She stood at the door, shoulders back, head up. "Ya know, you're wrong about me." And then she opened the door and walked out.

She walked slowly back down the corridor that just minutes earlier she had bounded along, hopeful that Catherine might have changed her mind. It was a long shot, but why else would Catherine want to see her? Now though, she knew better. Now she wanted the floor to open up and swallow her whole. Her heart beat in her chest, thumping out a melancholy tattoo with every step she took.

Passing the staff lounge, she didn't hear Amber call out her name. She didn't hear anything other than Catherine's words replaying over and over inside her head. *There is nothing between us and there will be nothing between us, what happened needs to be forgotten, do I make myself clear? Forget it, Brooke.* She felt sick. Her throat constricted and she moved quickly to the toilets. Flinging the door open to the cubicle, she made it just in time before the contents of her stomach emptied into the clean white bowl.

She retched, over and over, until her throat was sore and her eyes watered, and then she sank to the floor, crying like she hadn't done in years.

Chapter Twenty-One

Brooke returned home that night with heavy shoulders and aching heart. Dropping her bag and jacket on the floor by the door, she kicked off her shoes and padded quietly down the hallway. A radio was playing somewhere in the house, the tune upbeat and fun. Brooke scowled at the words of love being spouted by the female voice.

"Robin?" she called out. Her mood had not gotten any better as the day had progressed. Hours spent with Potter chasing around after people who had nothing more interesting going on than that they were actually shopping had worn her down.

She couldn't wait for Monday, when she would get her own radio and be able to patrol without Potter stuck to her side. That was if she made it to Monday and didn't die of a broken heart and mortification over the weekend. "Robin, get out here right now!" The volume on the radio lowered and her sister's door opened.

"Hey Brooke, thank god, I am starving!" She smiled. Passing Brooke, she moved towards the kitchen. "I made a shepherd's pie."

"Great, but I'm not hungry." Brooke tried to stem her anger. All day she had considered things, trying to fathom why Robin would do something so incredibly idiotic, and all she ever came back to was that she cared and wanted Brooke to be happy. She couldn't be angry at her for that, and yet, she was. Really angry.

"Oh, did you eat already? Well, it doesn't matter, I'll just let it cool and then it can go into portions for the freezer." Robin turned when she sensed eyes on her. She could literally feel the glare. "Brooke? What's wrong?"

The elder sibling rubbed a hand over her face before pushing her fingers into her hair and grasping at it by the roots. "What's wrong?" Her voice was even. Quiet even, considering. "Why? Why would you go to my place of work and speak to Catherine like that? Why, Robin? I just can't comprehend what on Earth possessed the pair of you to do that."

The youngster's face instantly blushed. Brows raised and her mouth hung open in disbelief. "She told you?"

Brooke raised her eyebrows. "Of course she told me, what did you think she was going to do? Call me up and say 'hey Brooke, I've been thinking about it and I miss you, let's give it a go?'"

Robin smirked hopefully. "Yeah."

Brooke shook her head. "No."

"No?" Now Robin was getting it. She looked worried.

"No, Robin, she didn't. It doesn't work like that when you're a grown-up." She ran her hands through her hair again. "Oh, she called me though. I had to go to her office and be reprimanded for basically stalking her."

Now Robin looked angry. "What? Why? You haven't stalked her."

This time Brooke rubbed both palms up and down her face, groaning loudly. "Robin, you can't do that, you can't make somebody like someone else, and you definitely cannot go to my work place and interfere like that."

"I'm sorry, Brooke. We thought we were helping. Dad always said that he wished someone would talk some sense into Mum and I just..." She burst into tears.

Forget it

Brooke sighed before she moved quickly towards her sister, gathering her up into her strong embrace and shushing her. "It's okay, let it out. It'll be alright, I promise." Their mother was the most selfish woman they knew. There was no excuse for it. She chose her own life over those she had brought into the world. She had a new boyfriend every year and a different place to live, parties to attend and money only to spend on herself. In the last ten years she had had more Botox than a celebrity. "I know you were just trying to help, and mum's an...well she's an idiot, we both know that."

"I didn't mean to ruin things for you," Robin sobbed against her chest, sniffing between words.

"I know you didn't, but...it's different when you're older. Anyway, maybe you did me a favour. Catherine isn't interested, she made that very clear, and I need to respect that."

Robin squeezed her tighter. "She doesn't know what she's missing."

Brooke smiled at the unwavering loyalty and kissed the top of her sister's head. "I know what, let's have a sofa night. You pick the movie and I'll go get some popcorn."

~FI~

For once, Brooke wasn't disappointed in the film choice. Robin had gone for an all-out action spy thriller, and they were both engrossed. They sat on either end of the couch, a blanket stretched out between them as their feet met in the middle.

"I was thinking," Brooke said, dipping her hand into the popcorn bowl, "it's December next week. We should get some Christmas decorations and put them up."

Robin sat up and grinned. "Can we get a real tree?"

Brooke looked around the room and considered all the options for where they could put one. "I guess if it's a small one."

"It's gonna be weird without Dad this year."

"I know, but ya know what, I think that just means we should celebrate it even more. We can set a place at the table for him."

Robin smiled before sitting back. "I'd like that, maybe we can put his picture there so it's like he is with us."

"Sounds like a plan to me." Brooke grinned. "And tomorrow we can go into Pollards and pick up some stuff."

Chapter Twenty-Two

After a fitful night's sleep, Brooke gave in and got up. Her subconscious had trapped her into a world where Catherine Blake had turned into her mother, something she really didn't want to think about. She rationalised that it was simply because neither of them wanted her in their lives, which made her sad, but at the same time she felt a prick of resentment too. It hurt.

She shuffled out into the kitchen in a pair of green boy shorts and a vest, shivering at the drop in temperature overnight. Flicking the kettle onto boil, she flopped down into a chair and sat in the dark. Elbows on the table, she let her head rest in her palms until she heard the faint click of the kettle as it reached its maximum potential. Dropping the teabag inside of the cup, she poured the boiling water over it, concentrating hard to make sure she didn't overfill it. Rhythmically, she stirred the spoon around the cup until she had a vortex of whirling water threatening to pull her into it and swallow her up, which was kind of preferable to what she was going through right now.

It was still dark outside, and the flat felt colder than ever. She turned the thermostat up a couple of degrees and took her tea into the living room, where she could wrap herself in the blanket from the sofa. It would look lovely in here once they had some decorations up. The radio stations had already started playing Christmas songs and usually that would be enough to get Brooke into the spirit of it all, but this year was different.

Her dad was gone. Just like that; one minute he got a diagnosis, and the next, heart attack, and not even sixty. The last time she had spoken to him, he had made her promise that if the worst happened, she would take care of Robin. She fully intended to keep that promise too, but the pressure to give her the life she deserved was high. She had to find the money for that school trip; it was hugely important. But at almost a thousand pound for a 5-day trip to Athens, it was going to be a stretch. And then there was Christmas; she would need presents and food. There was no way she was going to let Robin down.

The savings she had left would pay this month and next month's rent, plus some towards Christmas. After that though, they would be relying on Brooke's employment.

Pollards was a good job for now. They paid a lot more than many other security jobs did, and of course she got extra payments for unsocial hours that she would be working, but there wasn't going to be much left out of her wages once the rent and bills were paid.

She would just have to tighten their belt. If she bought their shopping daily from the reduced section, that would save a heap until she passed the six-month probation period and got her own store discount card. She yawned and swallowed down the rest of her tea.

Of course, the way that Catherine had reacted was now a problem. Brooke was under no illusions that that six-month period could be halted at any time, and Catherine was in charge of hiring and firing, so it didn't bode well that she had pissed her off. She wanted to hate the woman, but she couldn't; Catherine hadn't really done anything wrong. She would just have to do as Catherine wished: forget it and avoid her at all costs. She would keep her head down and just get on with the job, because when push came to shove, Robin was more important than her non-existent love life.

Forget it

Robin was excited as they entered the store and all of the lights dazzled her. Christmas songs played loudly over the speaker system and she started to sing along. Stan gave Brooke a nod as she passed, and she smiled back at him as she followed Robin.

"So, where ya wanna start first?" Brooke asked, pushing a trolley, which Robin promptly took charge of.

"Lights, we need lots of lights," Robin gushed. This had always been her favourite time of year. Brooke could remember the few times she had gotten leave over the holidays and how excited Robin would be. She was probably just six or seven when Brooke had left for her army training. She hadn't been home for Christmas for a couple of years, but that first time back had been memorable. Robin had followed her everywhere.

Their mum was actually still at home on that occasion, one of the last before she ran off with Terry from across the road (he didn't last long though before she came crawling back). Robin had been so excited when Brooke walked in carrying presents; it was probably one of the best memories Brooke had. They'd always been close, even with the 11-year age gap. Though as Robin got older, that gap seemed to feel less and less.

Robin raced towards the Seasonal aisle, pushing the trolley fast and then jumping up onto the back of it. "What about these?" she bellowed excitedly.

Brooke caught up and took the box from her hand, casually glancing at the price. They were expensive. "Maybe, but there are a lot in this box. I'm not sure we need that amount of lights for the size of tree we can fit."

Robin scrunched up her nose. "I guess so," she said, a little crestfallen.

Looking down at the section, Brooke saw the same style but in a smaller box. "Hey look, these will work. Exactly the same, but a lot less of them." Her kid sister's face broke out into a smile again.

"Yes. Now we just need tinsel and baubles. Did you consider a colour scheme?"

The laugh that bubbled up from Brooke's throat was the best sound she had heard for days. "No, Sis, why don't you decide?" Her joy didn't last long though; as soon as Robin was off again, Brooke was mentally calculating the cost.

~Fl~

Catherine was running late. She cursed silently under her breath; lateness was a habit she didn't intend to continue. But here she was, at Pollards for last minute shopping. She hadn't realised just how low her bottle of shampoo had gotten until she was packing for her weekend spa retreat. If there was one thing that she disliked most about hotels, it was those expensive-looking shampoo and conditioners they used. For some reason, her hair never felt right when she used them. She checked her watch again. If she was quick, she could be on the road in 10 minutes; and maybe, if the traffic was good, she could make up the time.

Only there was one slight problem to her plan: Brooke Chambers. She cursed again; what were the odds? Had she really been such an awful person that the Gods were so against her? She got to the one aisle she needed in the entire store, and the one person she was desperately trying not to think about was standing right there, right next to her brand of shampoo, looking all cute and casually perusing the brands without a care in the world.

Forget it

Catherine hid at the end of the aisle and pretended to be interested in the bright pink hair colour that was on a special that week. As she hovered, she couldn't help but watch Brooke and her sister interacting.

From her position, she realised that she could easily observe Brooke more closely. Unguarded, the brunette didn't appear to be having fun. A note of sadness and worry would descend upon her angular features anytime her sister moved away, magically disappearing the moment Robin returned. Brooke's face would then light up and Robin would grin in return, placing her latest item, always costlier than the one before, into the trolley. The trolley that was already filled to the brim with Christmas; they would be having a lovely time by all accounts.

Catherine wondered why that was. If Brooke was unhappy or didn't want the item, then why let her sister have it? Family dynamics were not something Catherine really understood. Being an only child to parents who were a lot older than those of most of her peers, she had been what she laughed off as an orphan for almost a decade. She didn't really celebrate Christmas, or any other event throughout the year. Only a handful of birthdays had been spent whilst in a relationship.

Eventually they moved off and Catherine took the opportunity to get what she came in for. She grabbed it off the shelf and then turned to retreat, but she couldn't help one last look back over her shoulder at them as they crossed the central aisle to continue on. She should have known better. Her eyes locked with Brooke for just a moment before the younger woman's cheeks reddened and she ducked her head, turning away.

Chapter Twenty-Three

Monday morning came around way too fast for Brooke's liking. Her first week anniversary apparently had to be celebrated, and Paul made a big deal of handing over the walkie talkie, going over all the rules again, testing her on protocols. She didn't want to point out that she had actually killed people for Queen and country and that Pollards rules and regs were a piss in the ocean compared to the Army. He was pushing her already-frayed buttons, but she relinquished her annoyance. It wasn't his fault she was in a foul mood.

After seeing Catherine in the store on Saturday, she suddenly realised just how difficult it might be to avoid her. She had no real idea what Catherine's job involved, or how often she left her office, went to the cafeteria, or wandered around the store. And of course, seeing her had set off the constant questioning of why Catherine was behaving this way. She had even come to the conclusion that Catherine wasn't even a bisexual, that it had all been a fantasy she had finally gotten to act out and then, reality kicked in and she wanted to forget it ever happened.

Robin told her she was an idiot.

She had her new shift pattern too, having now been officially added to the rota. There were the obligatory night shifts, which she kind of looked forward to. The store was closed to the public, but staff were in restocking shelves and moving displays, so there were always two security guards on duty during those hours. It would be less stressful, and definitely no chance of bumping into Catherine.

This week though, she would do four early shifts. Then she had two days off before another set of day shifts. Didn't seem too bad, she thought as she started to make rough plans in her head. She would even be home around the same time Robin got back from school, though the youngster would have to get herself up and off to school in the mornings. Yet again, Brooke was grateful to Yasmeen for picking up Robin and dropping both girls off on her way to work. She worked in the family business, just mornings. The Khans had three children, and Jas was the eldest. Krishna was twelve and the baby, Ishaan, was nearly two. So, she dropped Kris and Jas off in the morning and took Ishaan with her to work at the store.

"Now, remember, this is the time of year that we get inundated with tealeaves." Zoning out already, Brooke smirked to herself. "Keep ya eyes peeled and grab the little oiks," Paul was saying as they walked back out onto the shop floor.

~FI~

By Wednesday, Brooke just about had the layout of the store stamped into her mind. She knew each and every aisle number and what was on sale. She knew all the new displays and had already caught two kids trying to steal a couple of games. They were too dim to know that the cases were empty. So far, she had been spending her lunches with Amber, who had tried, unsuccessfully, to get out of her what it was that had made Ms Blake so mad the previous week. Brooke didn't think it was anyone else's business. She wasn't the type to gossip, and quite frankly, she really didn't want to admit how pathetic she was, nor did she think it fair to gossip about Catherine regardless of how unfair she had been. Kim and Amber had no idea her little gifts were anything more than just being nice. In the end, Amber stopped asking. Instead, they swapped phone numbers and agreed to meet up at the weekend for drinks. Brooke was looking forward to it. Maybe a night out with a friend would brush away the lingering interest in Catherine Blake.

The last thing she needed after lunch was to run around the store until she was almost blue in the face, chasing after Potter and his overly enthusiastic approach to security work. Mostly, he tailed perfectly well-behaved customers around, quietly intimidating them into heading to the tills as quickly as possible, but then he'd be off, charging around the store sniffing out someone who just happened to be wearing a baggy coat. He was exhausting to work with.

Brooke let him run as she wandered back and forth around the high-priced sections and the areas where people were most likely to attempt a theft. Surprisingly, beef was one of the most stolen items – that and hair products, razorblades, and alcohol. High-tech and high-priced items were always on the list for the common thief.

Currently she was patrolling aisle 7: dentistry care items on one side, hygiene products on the opposite set of shelves. An elderly gentleman was struggling to reach a can of shaving cream on the top shelf. His spine looked curved, and he had trouble raising his arm. "I'll get that for you, sir," she offered, stepping up beside him.

"Oh, thank you, dear. I do struggle."

She handed him the tin can. "There ya go, no problem at all." She watched him shuffle off and grinned. Maybe this job wasn't quite so bad.

The loud shrill of an alarm rang out across the store and her radio crackled into life, Potter's exuberant voice echoing through the channel to inform her of an attempted theft.

"Got a runner," he said. "Aisle one."

Turning on her heels, she ran, skidding to a halt at the end of the aisle, where she turned right and then left, hurtling past the baby products in aisle 4. It was difficult dodging around customers and trolleys, but finally she made it to the tills. She pushed harder and aimed for the front exit. From her right, she could see the blur of movement as something or someone hurtled towards the exit too. Sounds fell away as she concentrated on getting there first and stopping him or her from escaping with whatever it was they had grabbed and intended to steal.

There was a slowing of motion. She twisted her head to the right and saw the bulk that was heading her way. She was faster though, and would easily get to the exit before he did. Under his arm he still held onto what looked like a laptop with the alarm system wires still attached and dangling from it. Looking up, she made eye contact with him. He didn't slow. He didn't try to dodge. He was coming right for her with an malevolent grin on his face.

Planting her feet, she prepared herself for the hit. He dipped his shoulder and 300 pounds of muscle, bone, and fat hit her, lifting her off her feet. His arm grabbed around her waist as he rugby tackled her to the ground. She landed on her back with an almighty thump, and then her head hit and bounced off of the ground. All the air left her lungs in a loud "humpf."

And then it all went black.

Chapter Twenty-Four

"Brooke? Brooke? Can you hear me?" There was an angel speaking to her, a beautiful sound that filtered through her ears. Her vision was blurred, but she could just about discern the halo of gold that hung like a curtain around her face. She wanted to reach up and touch it, but good god was her head pounding. "Brooke?"

She heard herself groan. A sharp pain kept picking at her, like hot pins stabbing frequently. Still, it was all okay; the angel was smiling.

"Hey, just lie still."

Her head felt wet. Was it raining? Her thoughts were jumbled. With her right hand, she tried to reach up and feel her head, but something soft and warm took hold of it and placed it down across her chest, holding it there.

"Don't touch it, Brooke," the angel's voice said. Brooke's vision swam in and out of focus. Her angel was lovely, kneeling beside her and holding her hand. It would be heavenly if it wasn't for this god-awful pain.

"What happened?" she mumbled offhandedly. Her vision swimming in and out of focus made it difficult to get her thoughts together and made her feel nauseous.

"You were knocked to the ground by an oaf trying to steal a laptop." A man's voice this time. She looked up to find him hovering about her.

"Oh...where am I?" She tried to lift her head and look around. More people hovered over her. Why were they looking at her? Her last cognitive thought was of Robin, they had just moved into their new flat and were unpacking everything. How had she ended up here?

"Brooke? Don't you know?" The voice was like a gentle whisper against her ear. She felt her eyes closing again as another hand began stroking her forehead. It was nice, relaxing.

"So tired," she mumbled. Other voices now mixed in, but it was difficult to concentrate. She heard the words "ambulance" and "hospital" and wondered who had been hurt.

"Brooke, you're at Pollards Department store, you work here. You've had an accident and hit..."

"I don't have a job, I need one though." She chuckled and tried to open her eyes again. For just a moment her vision cleared again. "Wow, you're gorgeous."

~Fl~

Several hours later, Brooke was still in the hospital. Finally, her head had cleared a little; probably a lot to do with the drugs they'd pumped into her: painkillers, along with gas and air, or laughing gas – she was laughing quite a bit at nothing. She liked that stuff a lot.

She also had a little room all by herself, which was at least something. Sitting up in the bed, she looked around the room and tried to gather her thoughts. Why did she have a uniform on that she didn't recognise? She knew there were stitches in a gash to the back of her head and that someone had knocked her to the ground. What she didn't know was why? Why had someone hit her? Why was she in that store? She had as many questions as they did.

Apparently, they were not willing to let her go because she had a concussion? Oh, and she had a sprained wrist and contusions of all kinds. All in all, she was a little banged up, but she'd had worse. There was no reason to keep her here.

She sat there quietly and let them all fuss around her. They were all pleasant enough, and it wasn't like she had anywhere else to be. There was a little remote control attached to the bed. She pressed some buttons, and the bed tilted back until she was almost lying down. Tiredness kept coming and going. Releasing the button, she hooked it back onto the railing around the bed and spotted the clock.

Robin!

Her brain felt like it rattled inside her head, and a giant anvil dropped down on top of it when she sat back up far too quickly. She cried out in agony.

The door opened, and one of the nurses rushed in. "Brooke, what is it?"

"Someone needs to get Robin."

"Okay, just relax. That head of yours needs a lot of rest right now," she said, checking her pulse and watching the monitors. Politely, Brooke waited to get her attention and tell her about Robin, but the door opened again, and this time two men entered. She had seen both men before. The one in the uniform like her own had travelled with her in the ambulance. His name was Paul something, and the other guy was the doctor. She couldn't remember his name. They stood just inside the doorway and were joined by the nurse, listening as she filled them in on her latest observations.

"Hello, anyone? I need to get my sister!" she all but bellowed at them.

The tall man in the white coat looked at her and smiled, "Sorry, Miss Chambers, I just need to ask you some questions. Would that be alright?" He was a handsome guy, looked a bit like Dev Khan, only younger. His name tag read Dr M Rishne.

She huffed. "Yes, but you need to be quick, because I have to get home. My sister will be worrying where I am."

He smiled again. "No need to worry, I believe someone has gone to get her."

With that information, she felt herself relax a little until she suddenly realised that she didn't know anybody. "Oh, who?"

"I don't know, but I know that she should be here very soon." He smiled kindly. "So, Brooke, can you tell me what the date is?"

"Of course, it's October the 14th."

He wrote it down on his pad. "Okay, great, and can you tell me where you work?"

She squinted at him. What kind of ridiculous questions were these, anyway? "I don't have a job right now, I just left the army and I am in the process of getting a permanent job."

He scribbled away again. "And your address is?"

She huffed and rolled her eyes. "Look, I feel fine. I just want to go home."

"And you can, as soon as you can tell me where home is." His charming smile was losing its appeal.

"Fine, flat C, 202, Milton Court."

He nodded to himself and then stood up again. "I'll be right back."

She let herself sink back into the pillows and winced a little at the bruising. "Great," she muttered. "This is just great." How was she supposed to get a job in this state? Her eyes felt heavy again, so she let them close. She must have drifted off, because it felt like hours had passed. Confusion struck, however, when she looked up at the clock and realised it had been mere minutes.

"Hey, you're awake?" A familiar voice caused her to turn her head to the left.

"Robin, how did you get here?"

Robin leant forward and took Brooke's hand. "Miss Blake came and got me." She looked concerned as she stared down at her sister. "She said you hit your head and you can't remember stuff?"

"Pftt, I can remember stuff. I'm just a bit murky on a few things. What day is it?"

"December 3rd," Robin answered instantly. "The doctors think it's just a bad concussion, but they're concerned that it might be a retrograde..." She thought for the word. "Amnesia?"

Brooke nodded slowly and looked around the room, trying to gather her thoughts. "December 3rd? So, I've lost 6 weeks of my life, of my memory?"

Her sister nodded. "I think so. But they said it might come back."

Brooke tried to sit up and winced again. "Who is Miss Blake? A new teacher?" she asked, grabbing the remote and moving the bed back into a seated position.

Robin laughed out loud. "No, you..." And then she remembered how hurt Brooke had been about the whole thing. Maybe it wouldn't be so bad if she forgot about it. "...work with her," she said quietly.

Brooke rubbed her head and let her cheek rest on her palm once she was done. Blowing out a breath, she asked, "So, I got a job?" As she spoke, the door opened again, and a woman entered. A beautiful woman in a white dress. In any other situation, she might have taken Brooke's breath away.

"Yes, you work at Pollards." The woman spoke confidently, but the smile was shy, as though she wasn't sure it was the right thing to do.

Brooke held her stare and tried a smile of her own. She looked familiar, but Brooke couldn't quite place her. "Miss Blake?"

Catherine turned to Robin. "I thought they said she couldn't remember?"

"She can't," Robin said without looking back at the woman.

"You're the angel?" Brooke finally worked out why the woman looked familiar.

"I'm the..."

Brooke scoffed at how silly that had sounded. "Never mind, So, I work at Pollards?"

Catherine slowly released the breath she had been holding, "Yes, and of course, you don't have to worry about anything while you are in need of medical attention. Pollards has a very good insurance policy and maintains an outstanding record..."

"So, I'm getting paid while I am injured?"

"Of course, hurt in the line of duty as they say."

Brooke sighed, feeling relief that at least something was going her way at last. "Okay, so when can I go home?"

Chapter Twenty-Five

The stark bright white walls and the overhead strip lighting were enough to give anyone a migraine, let alone someone with a concussion. Surprisingly, the painkillers were knocking the edge off the pain; even the bruising down her back didn't feel as awful now.

She had managed to go to the toilet by herself, although Robin had had to undo the button on her trousers for her. It was a test. She had walked up some steps unaided; another test. There were no fractures in any of the x-rays. The only concern now was the concussion and the memory loss. Neither of which did Brooke see as reasons why she couldn't go home.

"I'd really rather you had someone with you for a couple of days at the very least," Dr Rishne explained from the edge of the bed, where he had perched himself. "Retrograde amnesia is a very serious thing."

"That's all well and good, but there isn't anyone, so...I'm a big girl doc, been in the army."

He smiled at that, but continued. "I'm just concerned, if you forgot to turn off the gas for instance."

Sitting back in the uncomfortable armchair, Robin piped up. "I can look after her."

Shaking her head, Brooke regretted the movement in an instant. "No, you need to go to school, I'll be fine."

"I really would advise..."

"I can do it." All heads turned towards the voice in the corner. "I can take leave, God knows I have enough of it left to take this year. The office will run fine without me. How difficult can it be?" When she finally finished speaking, she wondered if she was trying to persuade the doctors, Brooke, or herself. She avoided looking at Robin. She could feel the glare being sent her way.

Brooke clapped excitedly and pointed towards Catherine. "There, see, so we're sorted then? Can I go home?"

~Fl~

"I'll just go fetch the car," Catherine said, smiling awkwardly. Robin continued to glare, her arms wrapped around her torso to keep warm. It was cold outside the hospital entrance, an arctic blast of wind doing nothing to help.

Brooke smiled at her from the wheelchair they insisted she use. "Hey, thanks, but we're cool from here. Robin can call a cab."

Catherine clearly looked confused. "I thought that I was..."

"Look, I'm not going to hold you to that. You don't even know me. The last thing you need is to be stuck with a stranger for a couple of days. I'll be fine, honestly." She tried to stand up and almost fell over. Pain shot up her spine and she quickly became lightheaded.

Catherine and Robin both grabbed for an arm. "Woah, Sis, come on, at least let her take us home. It's the least she can do." She glared at Catherine as she spoke, but thankfully Brooke missed the unease between them.

"Fine." Brooke waved them both off. She was in too much pain and too cold to argue about it. "Fine. Robin, go with her, it's too cold to be standing here. I'm alright, I've got the blanket."

Robin huffed, but she didn't argue; it *was* cold. Plus, she had a few things she wanted to say to *Ms* Blake now that she knew Brooke was okay.

Catherine searched her bag and pulled a set of keys out ready. "Won't be long." She pulled her coat collar tighter around her face in an effort to ward off the freezing wind.

Robin waited until they were out of Brooke's earshot. She glanced back to make sure that Brooke wasn't watching before she turned and glared again. "Why are you doing this? It's a little mean, don't you think?"

"Actually, I thought it was a nice thing to do," Catherine replied offhandedly.

"Really? What, to flaunt yourself around her just so you can tell her to get lost again?"

Catherine stopped in her tracks. "Sometimes there is more to a story than you know," she offered simply before continuing on with her stride.

Robin doubled her speed to keep up. "If you're going to do this, then you need to make sure that she doesn't remember you."

Catherine glanced at her before turning back to check for cars so they could cross the road safely.

"You didn't see her," Robin continued with her protest, "It really hurt her the way you treated her. She didn't deserve that, and it wasn't even her fault. She didn't know what me and Jas were going to do. She didn't send us."

The older woman listened, but she remained silent. They were at her car, and all she wanted right now was to be warm. Robin would just have to suck it up. She hit the alarm button and the car doors unlocked with a loud click, indicators flashing orange. "Get in."

The stroppy teen yanked the door open and flounced in. "I'm just saying, if you have no intention of seeing her again, then don't bring it up, don't remind her about it."

"Alright," Catherine snapped. "Now belt up," she said, understanding the double meaning as she pulled her own seatbelt across and locked it into place. She put the car into gear and pulled away. "You know, I am not the monster you seem to think I am."

Robin cut her eyes at her and looked out of the window. "It doesn't matter what I think. I care about Brooke."

Catherine nodded. "Believe it or not, so do I."

The youngster scoffed. "Yeah, right."

They could see Brooke up ahead, just where they had left her. As Catherine pulled into the kerb, she added, "I will drop you both home and then go back to mine to pick up some things."

"Whatever," Robin said, opening the car door with a smile for Brooke.

"Ready to go, Sis?"

Chapter Twenty-Six

Brooke eased down into the couch, grimacing as she sank down onto the battered old cushions. The bruising was becoming more obvious as the day wore on. Dark reds and purples spreading out across her skin in various places reminded her of an ink painting Robin had made for her years ago.

"Thanks," she said, smiling through the pain as Robin helped pad her out with more cushions. "Good job you can cook, eh?" She laughed as her stomach rumbled. It was nearing 7 p.m. and she had no clue when she had eaten last. She assumed if she had a job now and had gone to work this morning that she must have had some breakfast, but she had no recollection on what it might have been, or if there was any lunch. "I guess we should wait for...what was her name?"

"Catherine, Catherine Blake," Robin answered pulling Brooke's shoes off. She glanced up to see if the name rang any bells with her sister, but it didn't seem to.

"Oh yeah, Blake...Catherine? That's a nice name, isn't it?"

"I guess." Accomplishing her task, Robin then turned towards the thermostat. It was chilly in the room. "Do you want a blanket?"

"Nah, I'm good, thanks though. Will you let me know when it's time to take my painkillers? My head is sore." She tried to shuffle about a few cushions, but couldn't quite manage it without Robin's help again. "Thanks."

"Stop saying thanks. You look after me, I look after you, right?"

Brooke nodded. "Right."

"I'll get some dinner on, wanna drink? I can make a pot of tea or, I think we have some lemonade left."

"Lemonade would be great." She went to say thanks again but caught herself at Robin's raised brow as she left the room. Brooke grinned and let her head fall back against the cushion. The stitches tugged a little, and she groaned.

~FI~

Catherine sat in her car outside of Brooke's flat, reminded that she had already been here twice before. Happier times. Her phone rang; Ronnie calling her back.

"Hen, what kind of garbled message was that?" She chuckled. When Catherine had dropped them off, she had called Ronnie in a panic.

"Jesus, Ronnie, this is not the time for taking the piss out of me."

"Woah, you're serious? You've volunteered to stay with this woman that you're totally into?"

She sighed. "Yes."

"Holy hell, are you a glutton for punishment or what?" Ronnie said. There was silence for a moment before she added, "What do you expect is going to happen here?"

"I don't know, I didn't think about it...I just..." She closed her eyes and shook her head. "I just wanted it to be me..."

"Sweetie, you need to decide what you want."

"I know, I know."

Forget it

~FI~

Robin returned almost instantly and pulled the small table closer before she put the glass down on top of a coaster. "Where is she going to sleep?"

"Hmm?"

"Catherine, where is she going to sleep?"

Brooke opened one eye. It was already weird that a complete stranger was going to be staying with them, but she hadn't considered sleeping arrangements. "I'll just stay here on the couch."

"You cannot sleep on the sofa, Brooke, I will. She can have my bed."

"No, Robin. You have school tomorrow and Friday. You're not giving up your bed."

The teen rolled her eyes. "Fine, well we need a solution before she gets back." The doorbell rang. Both sisters looked to the door and then each other. "I can stay with Jas."

~FI~

Brooke could hear their muffled voices as Robin let Catherine into the small apartment. There was a lot of hushed whispering, and at some point, she thought she heard Robin very clearly say no. She smiled to herself at that, her little sister being all protective. Of what, she wasn't so sure, but it was sweet anyway.

She reached out for the remote and flicked the TV on. A soap opera that she didn't watch was on, so she flicked through the channels until she found something that half-interested her. Her head was pounding now, and the bruising on her lower back hurt like a bitch.

Laying her head back down, she closed her eyes again and listened as the voices became louder and clearer. Something was rolling down the hallway, most likely Catherine's suitcase. The woman intrigued her. She was obviously nice; who else would give up their free time or take time off from work just so they could babysit a virtual stranger? She was attractive too, for someone older than herself. *We must be friends at work*, Brooke mused, *that must be it. Which means it will probably be really nice and a lot of fun to get to know her again.* Her thoughts scattered as she drifted off to sleep

When Brooke woke again, the room was in virtual darkness. The TV was still on, but the show she had been watching was long finished. Now, it was a documentary on penguins. She groaned as she tried to sit up and felt the stiffness from the bruising.

"Are you okay? Do you need any help?" A stranger's voice. No, not a stranger, she reminded herself. Someone she worked with: Catherine.

She licked her dry lips and tried to gather some moisture in her mouth. God, she hoped she hadn't been dribbling in her sleep. Her hand automatically wiped at the corner of her mouth at the crusty sensation of dried spittle. "I think I am okay. I just...how long did I sleep for?"

Catherine stood up and moved to squat beside her. She had changed clothing from earlier. Now, instead of the formal dress, she wore jeans and a sweater. She looked more casual and at ease as she smiled down at her. "Only an hour. Would you like something to eat? Robin left instructions on how to reheat the lasagne."

"Robin? Where is she?" She felt a little disorientated, like when you're in a dream and nothing really feels real. Catherine rested a palm on Brooke's knee as she used her strong thigh for leverage to stand back up again.

"She went to stay with Jasmine. Mrs Khan came and picked her up about twenty minutes ago." Her voice got louder as she neared the kitchen. Brooke could hear her pottering about in there, opening cupboards and drawers, searching for all the usual things but not knowing where they were. Plates clanked noisily before the beep of the microwave as it was set into motion. "I put my things in Robin's room. She said that would be alright."

Brooke looked up to see Catherine standing in the doorway, leaning against the jamb as she wiped her hands on a tea-towel. "Great, thanks for doing this. I feel a bit bad really, obviously we must be friends and yet, I don't remember you."

Catherine gave a quick smile. "We've only known each other a short while." She looked away, not wanting to be caught in a lie or say too much. Robin was probably right; what Brooke didn't remember couldn't hurt her anymore.

"Still. It's nice of you to do this, and once I do remember, I'll have to make it up to you." Brooke reached up and scratched at the side of head. That idea had given her a warm and fuzzy feeling that she didn't really understand.

"There really is no need, it's the least I can do. I don't think Pollards has ever had a member of security put themselves in the line of fire quite like that, certainly not in the time I have been there." *Or one that I have treated so badly.*

"So, I work as a security guard?" Catherine nodded, and Brooke continued. "When did I start?"

"Just last month." Catherine turned back to the kitchen as the microwave pinged. "A couple of weeks, really."

The information fitted into its new space inside Brooke's fractured memory. Just a couple of weeks? That wasn't very long at all. "So, do you work security with me then?"

She heard laughter. "Oh, no." Catherine continued to chuckle; the idea that she could work anywhere but human resources baffled her. "No, I am head of HR."

Now Brooke truly was perplexed. "So, I don't get it. How do we know each other?"

Catherine cleared her throat before answering. "We uh, well when anyone starts at Pollards, they have to...there is a procedure to learn all of the relevant SOPs."

"SOPs?"

Catherine smiled. Brooke had asked the same thing before. "Yes, Standard Operating Procedures. Lots of...health and safety mainly, and other documents about the workings of Pollards. So, you spent the first week in my office going through all of that."

"And in that time, we became friends?"

"Y-Yes," she stammered. The microwave pinged again and she disappeared back into the kitchen, grateful for the reprieve in questioning. When she returned minutes later carrying a tray, Brooke forced herself more upright and twisted her legs off from the sofa to the floor.

"Thank you," she said, reaching up and taking the tray from her. "This looks great."

Catherine smiled. "Robin said it was your favourite."

"Ah, yeah, I do like it. I try and encourage her, ya know? She loves cooking, so..." She shrugged. "But honestly, I'd rather have a stir-fry or..."

"Chinese," Catherine said without thinking.

The mouthful of food on the spoon stopped just shy of Brooke's mouth. "Yeah, how did you know that?"

"I'm sure you must have mentioned it," she deflected quickly. She turned her back and fled once more to the kitchen. This was going to be a lot harder than she'd thought.

~FI~

The need was getting worse. Brooke was sure she had felt this kind of uncomfortable situation several times out in the field, but right now it was embarrassing. She needed the toilet, but every time she stood up it would hurt, or she would feel dizzy.

She fidgeted about, her leg shaking as she tried to take her mind off of the fact that at any minute she would have to give in and ask for help.

From where she sat in the armchair opposite, Catherine couldn't help but notice the jittery movements Brooke continued to make. "Are you okay?" she finally asked.

"Yeah, I just..." Brooke wriggled about some more before finally giving in. "I need the toilet." She bit her lip and grimaced. "I just..."

Catherine stood up, "Why didn't you say?" She held her hands out and helped Brooke to her feet, holding her around the waist to steady her. They fit perfectly together as Catherine strengthened her grip on her hip.

"Okay to walk?"

Brooke nodded and shuffled her bare feet forward. Every step jolted a bruise somewhere. "Sorry, this must be so embarrassing."

"No, not really." Catherine's matter-of-fact replies helped to ease Brooke's humiliation a little.

Shuffling awkwardly down the narrow passageway, they reached the small toilet, both reaching for the door handle at the same time. When Brooke touched her, Catherine felt a tingling sensation that spread throughout her insides. She remembered just how she felt when this woman's touch had brought nothing but pleasure, and she yearned for it, but it wasn't to be.

Brooke leant back, letting the wall support her while Catherine rested one hand still at Brooke's waist, its warmth imprinting through her shirt. Brooke exhaled in relief when finally, she opened the door more fully. Brooke backed up and edged along the wall until she was inside the small space and then she realised a bigger problem.

"Okay?" Green eyes bore into Brooke's as she waited for an answer. Eyes that made Brooke's heart flutter.

"Could you, uh." She looked down and then back up, hoping that Catherine would understand. She didn't. She just stared back blankly, holding Brooke's pained gaze. Brooke held up her arm, her fingers bandaged together. "I can't...the button and zip."

Forget it

A perfectly shaped brow raised as understanding hit. "Oh. Right." Catherine stepped forward, toe to toe with Brooke, and reached down. Her hands between them, she tried to smile as she fiddled with the button. Brooke smiled back in an awkward kind of way, her good hand resting easily at Catherine's hip. "Fiddly," Catherine muttered under her breath.

"Yeah," Brooke agreed. Heat was rising in such close quarters. It had been a while since a woman had been this intimate with her. At least, she assumed so; she couldn't remember otherwise. Finally, task complete, Catherine looked at her.

"Uh, do you need me to..." Brooke nodded. "Right." She gripped the waistband of Brooke's trousers and underwear, and yanked gently until they were down by her knees. "I'll wait outside, I mean if you're okay to..."

"Yeah, I'm good." Brooke blushed as Catherine backed out of the room. "Fuck," she mumbled to herself, sitting down carefully.

Of all the times to find somebody attractive, it's when I can't go to the loo by myself, she thought with a silent groan.

Chapter Twenty-Seven

Chaperoned to her room, Brooke emptied her pockets and then let the pants drop to the floor. She managed to undo the top two buttons on her shirt and pulled that off too, tossing both items into the laundry basket.

Her room was tidy, as it always was. She was fastidious about it. Jiggling one of her drawers open one-handed, she pulled out a fresh top and some jogging pants. It was a bit of a struggle, but she managed to get her feet into them and gradually inch them up her legs. The top was easier. At least now if she needed help to go to the toilet, she could manage undressing herself. Though, she had to admit, it wasn't unpleasant being so close to Catherine. She had to also admit that there was something very attractive about her new friend. Shaking her head, she admonished herself for thinking that way about someone just trying to help her out.

On the bed, she noticed her phone, next to her wallet and keys. It had been in her pocket all day and she hadn't thought to look at it. Picking it up, she swiped the screen and noticed three messages all from someone named Amber.

Amber: OMG I just heard what happened, are you ok?!!

Amber: Please let me know as soon as you can, everyone is worried about you.

Amber: Okay, I guess you must be resting. Paul filled us all in, so I am glad you're alright. Are we still on for Saturday?

"Saturday?" Brooke repeated out loud. "And who is Amber?"

She made her way back to the living room and found Catherine now dressed in pyjamas. Brooke's confusion over Amber was now compounded by Catherine's bedroom attire. Little cartoon penguins dotted the material. She thought she had Catherine pegged as the typical office type following their first meeting at the hospital – she was a little ramrod straight and didn't look like she had that much fun in her – and yet, casual Catherine seemed a totally different prospect. Polar opposites.

"Everything alright?" Catherine asked, looking up from where she had curled her feet underneath herself in the armchair once more. She looked at home here, Brooke thought.

Brooke shrugged and gingerly eased herself back down onto the couch. She groaned as she bent and her back made contact with the cushion. "Apparently I have a date on Saturday with someone called Amber, but I don't remember who she is or how we met."

Catherine's eyebrows rose a notch, the look of surprise lasting barely an instant before she pushed it away and spoke. "Amber works in the office. She was the one that you spent most of last week with."

"Oh." She reached up and scratched her neck. "I had better reply then." Though she didn't know what to say really, she typed out:

Brooke: Hey, yeah, I am fine, thanks for asking. Remind me where we are going on Saturday?

She was hoping to get more answers than questions. She placed her phone down on the table and looked over at Catherine. "What's she like?"

"I don't really know," Catherine replied honestly, turning her attention back to the TV.

"But you work with her, right? In the same office?" Brooke continued. She literally had no recollection at all of who this Amber was or why she had agreed to go out with her on Saturday. Clearly, she must have liked her; otherwise she wouldn't have asked her out. That information put things into perspective regarding any attraction she had towards Catherine.

"I do, yes. Would you like another cup of tea?" she asked, standing up and heading towards the kitchen, which was rapidly becoming her safe haven to avoid difficult questions.

Shaking her head, Brooke replied, "No, thank you." She pushed herself up and followed Catherine. "Is she new too, then?"

Catherine reached for a clean mug and sighed. "Who, Amber?" She felt anger and humiliation poke at her senses. Or was it jealousy? Which was ridiculous.

"Yes, Amber, my date this Saturday."

"I think she has worked there longer than I have." The kettle boiled and Catherine added the hot water to the cup, keeping her back to Brooke, she closed her eyes and silently pleaded for her to stop asking these questions.

Her dark fringe flopped forward a little as she tried to work it out. Her thoughts were still pretty mushy right now. "But, didn't you say that you and I are friends?"

"Yes, I did...." She turned now, holding her mug of tea. "Are you sure you don't want one?"

"Yeah, I'm sure, thanks." Catherine edged past her back into the living room. "But I've only been there a couple of weeks. How can we be friends but you don't know anything about someone that's worked with you for longer?"

Catherine shrugged, sipped her tea, and winced at the heat, contemplating the truth as she placed the tea down on the table. But what would the truth bring? More questions that she didn't want to answer. "It's late, I think I might read for a bit in bed. Do you need me to do anything for you first?"

Brooke frowned. "No, I'm good."

~FI~

Catherine was lying under the unicorn-design duvet in a single bed, the likes of which she hadn't slept in since being Robin's age – and even then, Catherine was pretty sure she'd had a larger bed than this. Why on Earth had she volunteered to do this? It was so unlike her, so out of her comfort zone and yet, at times with Brooke, she felt more at ease with herself than she had in years.

Brooke was right though; she had known Amber for over a year and still didn't know a thing about her, or Kim, or anyone else she worked with other than what was in their file. She liked it like that, didn't she?

She turned over and bashed the pillow in frustration. "Dammit." Life was unfair. Meeting Brooke had been a highlight in her life. Brooke was somebody she had seriously considered allowing into her world: her home, her bed, her heart.

And now look what had happened. She had gotten her wish. Brooke had forgotten her and worse still, was going on a date with

Amber. "Fuck." They'd be dating and fawning all over each other in front of her. That thought alone hurt. She didn't want anyone else touching Brooke.

But then she considered how quickly Brooke had lined Amber up as a replacement. *What was that all about? Some play to make me jealous? Well, it's working,* she thought. *Or was I simply not that interesting to her once I was no longer a challenge?* She stared up into the darkness, her eyesight now more accustomed to it. *So much for our connection.*

She was jolted from her thoughts by a quiet knock. "Yes?" she answered a little timidly, or was it hopefully?

Brooke's head appeared around the door, "I just wanted to say thanks, again...for ya know, all that you've done. And you left your tea."

"Oh, thank you." Relief, or disappointment, washed over her. She wasn't sure which it was and which she preferred as she waited.

Brooke smiled as she wandered into the room and placed the cup down on the small stool Robin had by the side of the bed. The light from the hallway lit her up and just for a second, Catherine considered pulling back the covers and inviting her into bed. "Goodnight then," Brooke whispered.

"Yes, goodnight."

Chapter Twenty-Eight

Brooke barely slept a wink. The painkillers had worn off around three a.m. If she lay on her back, everything hurt. When she tried to roll over and lie on her side, everything hurt. Sitting up? Everything hurt. All of her muscles ached. It felt like she had been hit by a tank. Eventually, as the clock ticked its way past 5 a.m., she got up and went to make a cup of coffee.

Entering the kitchen, she almost jumped out of her skin when she found Catherine already sitting at the table, sipping coffee and reading a book. Something sinister by the look of it. There was a doll's head on the cover.

"Good morning," Catherine said brightly, lifting her glasses onto her head. She was dressed already too. Brooke wondered how she hadn't heard her moving around.

If yesterday she had been all business in her dress, hair up tidily in a bun at the back of her head and high heels on her feet, then now she was the complete opposite, and Brooke got the feeling that this was an image of Catherine that not many people got to see: jeans, with a rip across the right knee (not the ones she wore last night); a red t-shirt with a huge pair of lips on it that she recognised as Mick Jagger's; and the entire ensemble was topped off with canvas high tops. Even her hair was down, hanging loosely to frame her face. She looked gorgeous, and Brooke felt she already knew that fact about her, that she had already acknowledged it at some point before her memory loss.

"Morning." Brooke's voice was gruff and tired as she turned her attention away from Catherine towards the kettle. A feeling of déjà vu came over her, and she stored it away to think about later.

"Take a seat, I'll get it," Catherine said. She placed her book facedown on the table and stood up. Pushing her hair behind her ear, she asked, "Coffee, or tea?"

"Painkillers," Brooke grunted in response. Her head still pounded, and her eyes felt itchy and wanted to close.

"Goodness, that bad?" Catherine was by her side in an instant, helping her into a chair. "You don't look too good. Maybe I should call the doctor?"

Brooke pushed her hand through her hair and closed her eyes. Yawning, she mumbled, "Tired, pain, that's all."

Satisfied that she wouldn't fall off of her chair, Catherine set about getting Brooke's medication together. Easing the tap open, water gushed into the glass and she passed it across, watching as Brooke swallowed down the tablets and then finished off the water. She felt mesmerised watching the brunette lick her lips as she placed the empty glass down onto the table.

"Thank you," she said through another yawn.

"I think we should get you back into bed, you're dead on your feet."

Shaking her head, Brooke said, "I'll be okay. I'm gonna grab a shower though." Yawning, she stood up and stretched gently. "Might wake me up a bit, and the heat will help with the aching."

"Alright, don't get your hair wet though," Catherine reminded. The stitches needed to be kept dry. "And if you need anything, then just call me." Catherine took her by the elbow and guided her down the hallway. "I'll wait just here."

Brooke gave her a grateful smile and headed into the bathroom while Catherine stood outside, chewing her lip, listening to a string of curses and expletives as Brooke attempted to undress. Just as she was about to offer a helping hand, the shower came to life and she heard the creak of the door as it opened and then closed behind Brooke. Folding her arms, she leant back against the wall and thought back to the morning she had shared that space with her. Her face warmed as she remembered the details: Brooke down on her knees in the cramped space, peering up at her through hooded eyes as she brought Catherine to orgasm again. Her strong arms wrapped around Catherine's thighs, holding her and stopping her from collapsing as her legs gave way and her body succumbed to the inevitable.

She had been so engrossed in the memory that she hadn't heard the shower door open again. It was the bathroom door opening that brought her back from her thoughts. A dark head of hair poked out through the doorway. "Uh, so I have like a major problem." She grinned awkwardly.

"And that is?"

Her left arm poked out through the door. "What with the stitches in my head and this bandaged up, I am kind of at a loss on how to do anything."

"Oh."

"Yeah so, any ideas?"

"Let me think..." Catherine was a little flustered still. Just beyond that lump of wood was the naked body she had been thinking about, not just continuously for days, but specifically right now.

"Why are you up this early, anyway? Is Robin's bed not comfortable? She hasn't complained about it, but I guess it's a lot smaller than you're used to," Brooke rambled.

"I uh...it's a work day...I just woke up early out of habit I suppose." Catherine stuttered out a reply and tried not to stare at the water dripping down Brooke's clavicle.

"You get up this early on purpose?"

"Yes, I need the time to get myself ready for the office. Make-up, outfit...."

"You look great as you are," Brooke blurted out, and then blushed along with Catherine.

"This would not do for the office. Anyway, I like to enjoy a cup of tea and maybe read a chapter or two of my book. I like the quiet of the morning."

"Oh, makes sense I suppose." Before Catherine could continue to explain her daily morning ritual, Brooke steered the conversation back to the issue of the moment. "So, what if maybe if I tape a carrier bag around my hand, then I can wash and not worry about getting the bandage wet."

Catherine's eyes were drawn back to the hand, along the forearm attached, and up to the shoulder covered in flawless skin. She saw the odd freckle here and there and the fading tan lines of something very skimpy, according to how low they dipped on her cleavage. She hadn't noticed that during their night together, and she kicked herself for not paying better attention. She'd been too busy noticing other things. Like how she touched her as though she had been doing it for years. How her lips felt as they kissed a path down Catherine's stomach and sucked at the crease of her torso and thigh. She licked her lips at the memory of that first swipe of Brooke's tongue across her clit, remembering how she had arched into it and begged for more.

Brooke watched her, the way her eyes travelled her nakedness and she zoned out. "Or I can invite you in if you prefer," Brooke joked.

"What?" Catherine looked back up in alarm. "I...I'll get the bag."

Brooke chuckled at Catherine's departing figure. *She didn't say no,* Brooke thought.

Chapter Twenty-Nine

Amber: Anywhere you wanna take me!

"Well that leaves things open." Brooke chuckled to herself as she read Amber's text before she flicked to Robin's message, a warning to behave and not do anything she wasn't supposed to.

"Hmm, what does?" Catherine asked. She carried two mugs of coffee and a plate of biscuits.

Brooke looked up, reached for a mug, and set it down on the table next to her. "Oh, just Amber."

Catherine didn't reply and instead settled herself down in the armchair that had been her spot since she had gotten here. Brooke stared at her for a moment and wondered how it was that a virtual stranger to her could look and feel so comfortable in her home. She assumed they really must have hit it off at work.

"Can we go for a walk when we've finished our coffee?" Brooke asked. "I get a little stir crazy being cooped up all day."

"Sure, I guess we could do that." A walk would be nice. It was a little chilly, sure, but some fresh air would definitely blow away the cobwebs. "I don't have a coat though," she suddenly realised.

"I'm sure one of mine would fit."

~FI~

Catherine felt a little out of sorts all bundled up in Brooke's winter coat. The younger woman had insisted on a hat and scarf too, and it was a sensory overload. Every time she breathed in through her nose, she caught that faint fragrance of something

146

that was truly just Brooke. Like the delicate scent of apples in a blossoming orchard, it permeated the material and clung to Catherine, holding her hostage to it. The only thing she was grateful for was that it hid the permanent blush.

"So, Catherine, remind me about you?" Brooke asked as they strolled along the street outside. They'd taken a left out of the flat and were heading up towards the local park. It was not somewhere Catherine had been before; in fact, this entire part of town wasn't somewhere Catherine would usually frequent. As they had exited the building, she couldn't help the surreptitious glance over to where her car was parked; it was still there.

She pulled the scarf lower and away from her mouth in order to speak. "Oh, well uh...I like penguins."

Remembering the pyjamas, Brooke chuckled. "Why's that then?"

"I don't know, they're cute I suppose. A lot like me in..."

"Well you are cute, yeah." Brooke couldn't help but cut her off and flirt a little. There was something about Catherine that made that so easy to do, even if she was a little standoffish at times.

Catherine chuckled. "I meant, they're loyal creatures, they often mate with the same penguin each season. They're homey creatures too, preferring to stay where they know. Oh, I don't know," she laughed. "I just love the way they waddle."

Brooke grinned. "You should laugh more, it suits you."

Catherine raised an eyebrow. "How do you know that I don't?"

"That's true. You got me there." Brooke continued to giggle as they walked on. "Thank you." She spoke sincerely and stopped walking. "For doing this, I mean."

"It's only a walk. Does me good to get out; I missed my yoga class this week."

"No, I mean for all of it, staying with me. I'm sure I'll be fine if you have something better to do."

Something better to do than spend my time with you, Catherine thought. "No, there isn't anything better to do. I'll stick around till Saturday morning and then...Amber can take over." The thought of Brooke with someone else struck like a dagger. It was her own fault. She chose this path, didn't she? It was her choice to end things, to back away from any possibility of *it* happening again.

It had taken almost two years to find herself again and move forward as the confident woman that she now was. She wouldn't, couldn't, undo that on the whim of one night of passion with a woman that made her feel like a goddess. But it wasn't just one night, was it? *Oh god, I was an idiot, wasn't I? And now it's too late.*

They walked on some more in a comfortable silence. The sun was already low in the sky, shining off of puddles from an earlier shower. It was the kind of day when lovers strolled together arm in arm or hand in hand, and Catherine fought the urge to do just that. She could easily use Brooke's injury as the excuse, but what would be the point? Brooke had Amber. A scruffy dog ran past at speed, chasing after a ball, its owner trying to calm down the other pup that jumped excitedly by her side. They nodded a polite hello as they passed and continued up the slight incline that lead further into the trees.

"I love coming up here and just strolling around," Brooke said, breaking the comfortable silence.

"Yes, it's very relaxing," Catherine replied, smiling at the red nose and pink cheeks on Brooke's face. She could almost see what she would have looked like as a child. "I like the beach. Sometimes I'll just jump into the car and take a drive down to the coast. All that sea air, maybe we can..." She stopped herself mid-sentence as she realised what she was doing. She was being ridiculous.

"I'd like that," Brooke said, smiling at her. "If that was an invitation to go with you?" They stopped at a little café and lined up for hot drinks.

"Uh, yes." She felt a little stupid, like when she was a teenager asking a boy on a date. Changing the subject, she asked, "How's your head?"

Instinctively, Brooke reached up and touched the tender spot on the back of her head that had stitches, kept warm beneath her woollen hat. "It feels better now that the painkillers have kicked in."

"Good, and your hand?"

"Feels sore still when I move it." Brooke ordered hot chocolate and moved along the line.

"You were very brave to do what you did."

"What did I do?"

Catherine winced a little. She had seen the CCTV while Brooke had been taken to hospital and watched it again in slow motion with the police. It was a ferocious body slam to the floor. "Well, you managed to put yourself between the exit and a hulking great man intent on stealing a dummy laptop."

Brooke laughed. "Really? It wasn't even real?"

Catherine shook her head, still smiling. "I am afraid not. But he didn't know that, and neither did you, obviously. You raced to the doors and got there just before he did, and then he just kept running at you, he didn't even bother to try and dodge you." She shuddered at the memory. She had been in the cafeteria when she heard the alarm go off. Naturally, she had looked over the balustrade and watched in horror as it all unfolded. "He was at least twice your size, and he grabbed you around the waist and rugby-tackled you to the ground. I heard the crack as your head hit the floor."

"You saw it happen?"

"Twice. I was upstairs in the cafeteria. I'd just taken a seat by the railing when I heard the commotion downstairs. Just as I stood up to see what all the noise was about, I saw him take you down. And then obviously, I was there while the police watched the CCTV."

"Wow, can I watch it?"

Catherine recoiled in horror. "Why would you want to do that?" Brooke shrugged and they continued on.

The trees were bare, their leaves long since shed. Occasionally one or two leaves held on, grasping to the branch for as long as they could withstand the harsh cold breeze that whipped up as the afternoon began to move towards the evening. The sky was darkening with every step.

"You look cold." Concern etched across Brooke's features as she glanced towards her friend. Catherine shivered, but not just because she was cold. From the moment she had set eyes on Brooke across the floor of Art, she had felt the delicious shiver of arousal. It was still there, regardless of how much she tried to ignore it.

"Yes, a little." Now that the sun was setting behind the trees, it was becoming colder. That was the trouble with winter, and why she preferred the summer: 4 p.m. and it was virtually dark.

"Let's head back. I feel a little tired anyway. It's been nice though, just hanging out."

Catherine would be a liar if she said anything else. So, she just nodded her agreement and smiled.

~FI~

The flat was warm and cosy as Brooke opened the door and led the way inside. She could hear the familiar noise from the kitchen and knew that Robin was in there cooking something.

Catherine was the first to shed her jacket and scarf, and she headed into the kitchen, following the aroma of what she had to admit smelled delicious. What she didn't expect to find was a table laid for two, including candles.

"Hello," she said cautiously as she examined the scene. One brow rose as her eyes made contact with the chef.

"Hi," Robin said without looking over at the woman her sister had been infatuated with for more than a month.

"Something smells...nice. I'll get out of your way so you can enjoy dinner with Brooke."

Robin placed her dish inside the oven and closed the door. Looking up now, she rolled her eyes. "Mrs Khan is cooking for me, she's picking me up in 15 minutes," she said, glancing at her watch. "This is for Brooke and you, I only came back to pick up some stuff I need for tomorrow." She moved past Catherine and checked the hallway. Brooke wasn't there. "She doesn't remember you being a complete cow to her, so now you have the chance to make things right. Give her a chance," she pleaded in a half-whisper, half-hiss. "She liked you, all she wanted was a chance, and don't give me that crap about work, cos she told me that wasn't true. She read the SOP."

"I thought you wanted me to pretend nothing ever happened?" Catherine whispered back. "You don't even like me."

Robin checked over her shoulder again. "If she liked you, then there must be someone nice inside that she saw...even if the rest of us don't," she added with a sneer.

The harshness of Robin's word stung, but Catherine had to concede maybe there was some truth there. "She's seeing somebody else," she found herself confiding. Her shoulders sagged and she leaned back against the countertop. "So, thank you, but all of this is wasted on me."

Robin's face scrunched up. Brooke hadn't mentioned meeting anyone else. She had been mooning over Catherine for ages. She didn't say anything, but Robin knew her well enough to know when Brooke was over someone or still brooding, and she was definitely brooding. But more interestingly, Catherine hadn't said *she* wasn't interested.

"Right, you're just giving up then?"

"What?"

"I said, that's it then? Seriously, she's seeing someone else? No way. And if she is then it's nothing to worry about, because she's so into you...well she would be if she bloody well remembered." She stopped talking abruptly when they heard footsteps shuffling down the hallway. Brooke stepped into the room and found the pair of them standing in an awkward silence. "Hi Brooke, how ya feeling?" Robin said quickly.

"Yeah, okay thanks. Starving though."

"That's good." Her phone buzzed and she picked it up to read the message. "Right, Shepard's pie is in the oven. Needs another 25 minutes. Salad in the fridge. That's Mrs Khan outside, I'm eating with them tonight and tomorrow, but I'll be back Saturday morning." She kissed Brooke's cheek before turning and adding, "Bye Catherine."

In an instant she was gone, leaving a perplexed Brooke and an embarrassed Catherine facing one another over a candlelit table for two.

"I'll get the kettle on."

~FI~

Catherine had her feet tucked up underneath herself, her left arm leaning on the arm of the chair as she watched something on the television. Brooke, though, was more fascinated with watching her than anything the TV could offer.

Dinner had been awkward and left her feeling confused. Somewhere in her mind she knew the answers, but it just didn't register yet as a cognitive thought. She was going to have to have words with Robin, try and find out why it was that she thought a candlelit dinner was appropriate. So far, whenever she had seen

Robin and Catherine together, she had detected just a hint of dislike from her sister. She wanted to know why, and why the sudden turnaround in cooking for them.

"I'm sorry about dinner," she finally said after mulling it over for 20 minutes. "I don't know where Robin got the idea that there was anything romantic between us." She chuckled. Not that she wouldn't mind. Catherine was just her type; she hadn't forgotten that much. And the more time she spent with her, the more she wanted to get to know her. But then she would remind herself about Amber and get all confused about her feelings again.

"It's fine. I'm sure she just got me mixed up with Amber," Catherine said with a quick smile that disappeared as she turned back to the TV.

"Yeah," Brooke replied, sounding anything but convinced. This whole Amber thing was confusing too. For someone she was supposedly dating, she hadn't been that heavy on the communication. Other than the initial texts to see if she was okay and to check about Saturday, there had been radio silence. She hadn't even visited, or sent flowers. Nothing. But then she surmised that she had only known her for a matter of days, so maybe she was expecting too much.

Physically, she was feeling much better already. She hadn't even needed Catherine's help to go to the toilet, having made the wiser choice of elasticated waisted joggers as her preferred attire. Now though, she considered how she actually missed that close contact. She liked Catherine's hands on her, the warmth of her body pressing against her as she helped her move around. It was nice.

"You don't sound too convinced." Catherine's words brought Brooke from her thoughts.

"Oh, well I guess...I dunno, I've only lost a few weeks' memories. They just seem to have been quite important: meeting Amber, starting work, new friendships building." She smiled at Catherine. "But I can't help feeling like there is something else. Something important that I should know."

"I am sure it will come back to you, though maybe by then it won't matter." She could only hope that was the truth of it.

"Yes, you could be right." A half-smile graced Brooke's face. "What are we watching?" she asked, turning her attention back to the TV.

"A period drama...I'm not really watching it, if you wanted to switch over."

Brooke shook her head and stretched out her legs on the sofa. "Nah, I don't really watch TV much. I was thinking though, do you not have a boyfriend or someone you need to get home to?"

"My last boyfriend was five years ago. There's nobody else to be home for," Catherine answered. "I don't even have a cat. Just me."

Brooke nodded. "No one special on the horizon then?"

Catherine sighed; the irony. "I thought there was, not so long ago. I met someone who in a very short space of time turned my head, and I wanted to see where that led, but unfortunately circumstances meant that it wasn't meant to be. It's my own fault; fear I guess of the *known*." She chanced a glance at Brooke. Did she know she was talking about her? Had she worked it out? Was her memory returning? No, she just sat there looking back, her face interested but impassive. "It was someone at work."

Now Brooke's face took on a look of real interest. "Oh, and that doesn't..."

Catherine considered the options. She could carry on down the path she had chosen, come clean, or at the very least explain who she was and how she became this person. Maybe then, if Brooke ever did remember things, she might have a better understanding, be more forgiving. "A few years ago, I met someone at work and we had an affair that led to a relationship. Everything was wonderful, until the day that it suddenly wasn't...we broke up, and life for me became unbearable. I became the subject of office gossip; terrible rumours went around. People stopped talking to me, taking sides. It got so bad that in the end I left and swore there and then that I would never get involved with anyone at work ever again."

"Wow, that's horrible. It's a good thing you don't work with people like that now. He clearly didn't deserve you." Brooke said. She grimaced as she tried to sit up, and Catherine jumped to her feet to help. Putting her arm around Brooke, she eased her upright. "But maybe this new guy isn't like that either."

Catherine didn't amend the pronoun mistake; it didn't matter. "They're not, they're the most considerate, gentle, and honest person I have met in a long time."

"So, why not give it a chance. Take things slowly I guess, but why miss out on the chance of happiness if you could have it?"

"I should have...It's too late now anyway. They're seeing somebody else."

Chapter Thirty

Friday morning brought with it a scattering of snow. It laid for all of an hour before it melted away, ready to be forgotten by lunch time.

Brooke grabbed her phone. She needed to speak with Robin while she remembered.

"Is everything alright?" Robin asked, an urgency to her tone.

"Yeah, everything is fine. Catherine is looking after me." She moved the curtain slightly and looked outside: dull and grey.

"Good, what do you want then?" she said in that way only teenagers could. An uninterested but friendly kind of way.

Brooke turned back to face her room, the bed unmade and clothes scattered. She hated the mess. "Just checking in. Dinner was nice, thank you. But no need for the candles next time, eh? It was a little awkward. Catherine isn't my girlfriend."

"She could be," Robin pushed. She was still unsure of Catherine, but Jas had reminded her that Brooke liked her, and she wanted Brooke to be happy.

"No, she can't. She's kind of into someone else and anyway, she isn't gay."

Robin burst into laughter. It was actually ridiculous, and she wanted to bang both their heads together, except that would probably not be good for Brooke. They both thought the other was interested in someone else. Where they really this dense?

"What are you laughing at?"

"Nothing, sorry...go on." They needed to work this out by themselves.

"So, what's new with you? Mrs Khan fed up with you yet?"

This time, Robin chuckled. "No, she thinks I am great and said I can stay as long as I want. I think she wants to adopt me and fatten me up. Her food is amazing, she's teaching me how to make authentic Indian curries. Last night I helped make chapatis." She sounded happy, and that made Brooke smile. "So anyway, I'll be home early in the morning to get changed, and then I'll see you on Sunday I suppose."

"I thought you were back tomorrow?"

"I...the school Christmas disco is in three weeks, Brooke, and I need a new dress. Which is why we agreed that I could work at Mr Khan's store in the lead-up to Christmas."

"Well, I don't know about any of this, do I? I thought you were coming home on Saturday?"

"I am, to get changed."

Brooke sighed. There was so much she didn't know. Important things. It was getting more and more frustrating. "Ok, don't sneak in and out without seeing me first, okay?"

Robin laughed again. "Sure, see you later."

~FI~

Catherine took a call herself while Brooke was out of sight. She rolled her eyes at the voice on the other end of the line. Did she really have to do everything herself?

Ending the call, she put the device back inside her pocket, wandered back out of the lounge, and stood patiently in the hallway outside of her room, waiting. Yet again, Brooke didn't seem to have a problem opening the door while half-dressed. It unnerved her. She felt the instantaneous urge to place a palm against her chest and push her into the room, back her up until she fell backwards onto the bed, legs splayed to accept the warmth of Catherine's body pressing up against her.

"Good morning. I know this is just so inconvenient but, something has come up at the office and I need to pop in and organise it."

"No problem." Brooke smiled, opening the door a little wider. Now Catherine had no way of avoiding the black boy shorts and matching sports bra Brooke wore, or the toned torso, muscular thighs, and powerful biceps. She felt her mouth dry and had to swallow several times before she could speak.

"I don't want to leave you by yourself, is there anyone else you can call?" She kept her eyes firmly above chest height; safer ground.

Brooke shook her head, oblivious to Catherine's discomfort with her nakedness. "No, not really, but honestly, I feel fine."

Catherine seemed torn. "Maybe you should just come with me?"

Brooke found it quite a turn on that she cared so much. "Look, why don't we swap numbers and then you can call me any time, or I can call you if I need anything."

Catherine thought about it. It made sense she supposed, so she handed over her number, aware that they'd done this before

— the only difference being, she still had Brooke's number stored in her phone's contact list. "I won't be long. I'll pick up something for lunch," she said, grabbing the coat that Brooke had lent her the day before and heading out.

Biting her lip, Brooke thought some more about the woman who just left. Something was tugging at her subconscious. She liked Catherine, she was sure of that, but there was something more there.

The doctors told her not to try and force it; her memory would fix itself if it was going to.

It would come.

Chapter Thirty-One

Pollards was busy enough. Catherine strolled through the store and used her ID card to gain entry to the offices upstairs. HR had grown too large for the space it was squeezed into now, so they were being moved in the new year. Well, she was. Her office would now be along the hall, and the partition to her old office would be removed so they had more space. Kim and Amber would be getting new workspaces and a whole load more filing cabinets to fill.

Of course, she had forgotten about all of this the minute she saw Brooke hit the floor. She cursed herself now. She was being ridiculous, acting like a teenager in love. She wasn't in love. But she did like her...a lot. *Offering to stay with her and nurse her,* she scoffed at herself, *what was I thinking?* And yet, there she was two days later, getting to know Brooke even better than she had previously, and finding that she liked her even more.

She marched into her office with all the authority she could muster. Amber wasn't at her desk, but Kim was.

"Oh, Ms Blake, they said you wouldn't be in this week?"

Catherine stopped moving and turned to Kim. "No, I had something urgent come up. But I'll be in my office for the next..." she checked her watch, "hour, maybe less."

"Righto." The older woman smiled. "I'll let Amber know when she gets back from Payroll."

"Just...Carry on as you were, pretend I'm not here."

"Sure, Ms Blake," Kim said, already going back to her work on the computer.

Catherine was about to walk away when something stopped her. An idea was forming from something Brooke had said. Maybe it was time to stop living in the past. "Catherine."

Kim looked up. "Sorry?"

"My name...it's Catherine." With that announcement, she moved speedily into her office.

~FI~

The empty boxes had been piled up to one side. She needed to pack up anything that she would be taking to the new office. One by one she began to fill them up. She emptied her three-drawer desk first, followed by the four-drawer unit that housed all of the stationery she liked to use. There was a knock on the door. As she looked up, she caught a glimpse of Brooke's coat hanging on the hook and smiled to herself. "Come in."

Amber came into the room looking a little nervous. "Hi...Catherine." She said the name as though she was just trying it out and would be told not to do it again. "I bought you a cup of tea."

"Oh, thank you, Amber. Most kind. Please..." She looked around at the mess. "Just put it wherever you can find some space." She smiled, at least she thought that was what she had done, but the look on Amber's face meant she wasn't quite so sure.

"I wondered if you'd heard anything from Brooke, how she is doing?"

"I believe she is doing very well," she replied through almost-gritted teeth.

~FI~

Brooke was using the alone time to enjoy a bath. The hot water soothed the aches, and it would help bring the bruising out. Chucking in a liberal amount of bubble bath, she planned on luxuriating for a couple of hours with a book. Her planning had gone as far as to bring supplies in with her. There was a glass of juice, an apple, and her mobile phone, as well as a bar of chocolate that she had forgotten all about hiding in the back of the fridge.

She lay back and sunk down low, submerging herself in the water right up to her neck, though her knees popped out like suntanned mountains. She was lucky in that she had gotten her mother's skin tone. A little Mediterranean sun-kissed, their mother had always believed the family lore that a rich Italian had come across and swept their great grandmother off of her feet, resulting in the illegitimate spawning of her father. It was highly unlikely, Brooke thought. Having seen photographs of her grandfather and great grandfather, she knew they were the double of each other. Robin, on the other hand, had taken more of their father, pale and wiry. Thinking about Robin led to thoughts of Yasmeen, Mrs Khan. She considered that she really should thank her.

Picking up her phone, she swiped until she found Yasmeen's number and listened as it rang and rang. She was just about to give up when she heard the harried "Hello."

"Uh, hi, Yasmeen?"

"Yes, it's me, hi Brooke. How are you feeling?" she asked, just a hint of an accent detectable.

She stretched her legs out and pushed her torso out of the water. "Pretty good now, thanks. I just wanted to thank you for having Robin over."

"Oh, that's no problem, she is such a good girl. Good influence for our Jasmine."

"Yes, she is. You're still okay for her to stay tonight? You sound rushed off your feet."

"Bloody Dev, he has sprung a business meeting on me last minute. I'm running around like a blue fly trying to get dinner prepared. The little one doesn't want to take a nap, of course." Brooke chuckled at the way Yasmeen left out the arse of the blue fly. "But all will be fine, I am bloody superwoman." She giggled. "Don't worry about Robin, you get better and when she comes home, I'll send some of my famous chickpea curry."

"Thanks, I love that. You really should think about selling the recipe."

"Never, been handed down for generations, I'd be an outcast if I gave away the family secrets." She laughed again, and Brooke could hear the baby crying in the background. "Anyway, must dash, take care and don't worry about Robin."

She disconnected the call and sank back down into the water. Closing her eyes, she relaxed and let her mind wander its own path. Images floated past of Robin cooking in the kitchen, followed by Jas and Robin singing along to a TV show Brooke had never watched. The scene changed and a bar with paintings flashed across her mind. Music in her head played louder, a song she was sure she knew but couldn't recognise. There were flashes of a woman naked. The images were blurry still. She opened her eyes and rubbed at her face. Had she been sleeping with Amber?

She felt like if she had, then she would have some feeling towards the name.

The vibration of her phone against the wooden toilet seat broke her from that thought. She glanced at the screen and saw the name Catherine.

"Hey, all okay?"

"Yes, well...it's all a mess." She laughed and Brooke smiled. "In all honesty, I think I am going to be another hour."

"Alright, I'm fine. Take as long as you need. But don't forget lunch. I am starving."

"Oh, shall I send something round?"

"No, no, I'm fine, really. I've got an apple."

"Where are you, it sounds like an echo."

"I thought I'd jump in the bath for a bit." There was silence on the other end of the phone. "Catherine?"

"Yes, sorry, I'm here." More silence. "Please be careful."

"I will, so...I'll see you about one-ish then?"

"Yes, I think so. Bye, Brooke."

Catherine closed the phone call and opened her eyes. Images of a naked Brooke Chambers covered in bubbles, her skin damp as the steamy room brought a sheen of sweat, floated around in her head.

She sat down in her chair and leant her elbows on the desk, cradling her head in her palms. "What the hell is wrong with me?"

she said aloud to the empty room as she ran her hands through her hair and pulled it all into a tight ponytail.

Brooke was now seeing Amber, she had to get a grip on this and remember that. She threw her own chance away, and she highly doubted that when Brooke got her memories back that she would be even remotely interested anyway. Not after the way she had behaved towards her. She needed something, or someone, to take her mind off of Brooke, fast. Looking across her desk, her phone drew her attention.

Scrolling through the numbers, she stopped when she reached the one that she wanted.

"Hello, Ronnie, it's Catherine."

"I can see that, you alright?"

"Yes, I'm good, thanks. You?" She listened as Ronnie went into a diatribe about life and circumstances. "That's...well that's great. So, I was wondering if you were free tomorrow night?" Again, she listened while Ronnie went through every appointment in her diary.

"No can do, Hen. I have a very important date with the delectable Debbie." Her latest fling. Catherine rolled her eyes. Delectable Debbie wouldn't be around next month.

"Oh, that's a shame."

"But, if you were looking for a little something to take your mind off of all things Brooke-shaped, then I know a certain someone who is desperate to meet you again."

"Oh, who?" She was wincing before she even asked the question.

Forget it

Ronnie chuckled. "Petra. You remember her? Well she was very taken with you, always makes a point to ask after you."

Petra was nice enough. She wasn't someone who Catherine would usually give her time to. Though to be fair, Catherine didn't give her time to many people. But she needed something, or someone, to take her mind off of Brooke and Amber. "Alright, give her my number."

She placed the phone back in her bag and smiled to herself. A night out with this Petra would hopefully do the trick.

Chapter Thirty-Two

The water was going cold again. Brooke had already refilled it twice, luxuriating and allowing the heat to bring out the bruising, but now, as her skin wrinkled and she started to shiver, she considered whether she really should just get out. Checking the time on her phone, she realised that Catherine would be back in 15 minutes, and she wanted to be dressed and ready to have lunch. Her stomach had been seriously grumbling for the last 40 minutes.

She pulled the plug, watched the water begin to spin its way down the plug hole, and got ready to lift herself – and that was when she realised the problem. Her sprained wrist couldn't support her enough to push up, plus her painkillers were wearing off. She tried lifting herself with just her right arm, but regardless of her strength, it was impossible. Her feet kept slipping. "Shit."

The water had emptied, and the room was getting cooler. She shivered as the slight breeze from the open door chilled her skin. Trying again, she twisted slightly to put all the weight onto her right side, but that just caused the pain in her back to worsen. "Shit, shit, shit." Frustration and the knowledge that Catherine would be walking through the door any minute were not helping the situation. "Okay, think." This was not how she had envisaged her relaxing bath ending.

Once more, she tried lifting herself out using her right arm. Putting all of her energy into it, she lifted and was almost up enough to use her legs for leverage when her foot slipped and she landed hard on her backside, hitting the already bruised area with a thud. "Ow, fuck!" she cried out.

"Brooke?" Catherine's voice called out. "Brooke, are you alright?" her voice urgently called again as she rushed down the passageway.

"Yes," Brooke said, before groaning, "No, I'm stuck. I thought I'd be able to get out but, my wrist...I can't put weight on it to lift myself up." She reached out, grabbed her towel, and laid it over herself just in time for Catherine to appear at the open door. The sight of her made Brooke laugh out loud. She had one hand clamped over her eyes and was using the other to feel her way into the bathroom. "You can open your eyes. I'm decent, kind of..." Brooke grinned.

"I heard you cry out, did you hurt yourself?"

"More my pride, but yeah, I slipped and landed on my ars...bruise."

Catherine started to giggle. The more she laughed, the more Brooke couldn't help but join in. "I guess we should get you out, you must be freezing."

Assessing the situation, Catherine decided that the best way would be for Brooke to lift with her right arm while she hooked under her left and hoisted. She got into position and closed her eyes again. Brooke smiled at the gesture. As they worked together, the first thing that happened was that the towel fell away, revealing all. "Okay?" Catherine asked.

"Yeah, just got to grab..." She leant down and picked up the towel. "The towel." Wrapping it around herself, she sighed in relief. "You can open your eyes now." Catherine did so, then held out her hand once more to help Brooke climb out of the bath and onto the mat.

"Do you...I mean, are you alright with..." Catherine gestured to the towel and let her eyes slowly descend, knowing full well exactly what was hidden underneath.

"Oh, yes, I'll be fine getting dressed. I'm almost dry already," Brooke said, teeth chattering.

"Alright, I'll get lunch on the table. Just call if..." Her gaze held with Brooke. She didn't care about leftover Sheperd's pie or the salad and garlic bread she had picked up to go with it. She wanted to stand right here, just looking.

"I will."

~FI~

When Brooke reappeared in black leggings and a loose-fitting hoodie, Catherine had lunch served at the table, minus the candles.

"This looks nice," Brooke said as she took a seat, gingerly letting her back rest against the chair. Catherine pre-empted the issue and placed her painkilling medication on the table, alongside a glass of water. "Thank you."

"Quite alright." Catherine smiled and took the seat opposite, just like she had yesterday. It felt all so domesticated, as though this was her usual routine: returning from work to have a meal with her lover. Only Brooke wasn't her lover, not now.

"I was thinking," Brooke said between bites of food. "What's going to happen on Monday?"

"Monday?" Catherine said before taking a bite.

"Yeah, I mean I know now that I have a job at Pollards, but I don't really know what I do..."

"You don't have to worry about that, take some time off to get well."

"I am well, I mean, I'm not ill. I can come to work...I just don't know what it is that I do on a daily basis."

Catherine put her fork down and stared across at Brooke, incredulous that she was even contemplating coming back to work so soon. "Your job is very...strenuous, lots of time being on your feet, dealing with very awkward situations. There is no way that Pollards will allow you back so soon, it's just not possible. Plus, you will need re-training, reading through all the SOPs...literally everything you did these last couple of weeks is gone." She picked up her fork and continued to eat while Brooke considered things.

"So, why can't I do that?"

Catherine took another bite of her lunch. "Do what?"

"All my training? I'll have to do it again at some point. I can sit in an office and read stuff."

Catherine sighed. "Don't you want to just enjoy some paid leave?"

Brooke shook her head. "Not when there is nothing wrong with me."

"Brooke, you had a very nasty bang on the head. I really think..."

"Catherine, don't you think I'd be a lot safer if I was at work...with you watching over me?" She had a point. She knew it, and so did Catherine. It was a point that Catherine wanted to make herself, but she felt selfish in doing so.

"I don't know..." She did know. She had the say-so over such a thing. It was her decision; all she needed to do was have a quick chat with occupational health and voila, Brooke would be at work on Monday and under her supervision.

"Oh, come on, please, Catherine. I will be so bored here all by myself."

"Fine, I'll speak with Occ Health and see what they say, but..." She held her fork out and pointed it at Brooke. "If – and it's a big if – but if they allow this, then you will do exactly as you're told. No heroics, no pushing yourself too hard."

Brooke grinned and ripped off a chunk of garlic bread with her teeth. "No problem." She rather liked bossy Catherine.

Chapter Thirty-Three

Occupational Health agreed that Brooke could return to work under several stipulations. One, she wasn't to undertake her usual hours or position. Two, she was to spend only 1 hour at a time sitting, then she was to take a short break. If at any time her pain levels worsened, she was to go home. And three, if at any time Catherine felt that she was overdoing it, then she would be sent home.

Brooke agreed to it all. If she was going to get her memory back, then she figured the best place to do it would be by submerging herself in the very place she lost it. And if it didn't return, well at least she would be re-learning what she needed to know. It was a win-win as far as she was concerned.

"Did you want to watch anything in particular?" Catherine asked as they settled down for the evening in front of the TV.

Brooke shrugged. "Not really, did you want to watch something?"

"Oh, no, I just figured...usually I'd read."

"It's Friday night, don't you go out with friends or...someone more—"

Catherine interrupted quickly. "No. I'm quite the homebody really, my friends are...acquaintances really. There is no one special," she reiterated. Realising that she was on the verge of rambling, she laughed. "Sorry, too much information."

Smiling, Brooke shook her head. "No, it's nice. I'm getting to know you again, I suppose. So, single by choice then?"

"Uh, yes I suppose so." She smiled sadly, recalling this some conversation previously. "There was someone as I said, at least I thought maybe...but it wasn't meant to be." She looked away wistfully.

"That's a shame, I reckon you'd be a real catch for the right person." She noticed Catherine didn't say he. "What happened?"

Catherine scoffed at that. "Oh I..."

"Sorry, that was rude of me. I'm just, I'm not sure what I can and can't ask...we haven't known each other long, but I feel like...I feel as though I know a lot about you, I just can't..." She grimaced with frustration. "I can't quite get it...it's like it's there but out of reach to me."

"No, it's fine. Ask anything you want to. I'm an open book." *An open book? Where did that come from? This wasn't how things were supposed to be going.*

"Alright, let's play 20 questions. I'll go first," Brooke said, fidgeting so that her legs were pulling up under her. "Favourite colour?"

"I'm not sure that this is 20 questions, but okay, I will play along." The corners of her mouth twitched. "White, though I don't think that is actually a colour, is it?"

"Doesn't matter, go on, ask me a question now."

"Alright, what was your favourite subject at school?"

"PE. I was the sporty kid. If there was a sport to play, I was on the team. What's your favourite song?"

"Oh, that's a tough one. Probably something by the Carpenters."

Forget it

They batted questions back and forth. Each time Catherine answered, Brooke became more enamoured.

"When was the last time you got your heart broken?" Brooke asked. Sitting back now, she pulled the blanket up over her legs. When Catherine didn't answer right away, she assumed she had pushed too far. "Sorry, was that too personal?"

"A little, still burns I guess," Catherine said without explaining further.

Chapter Thirty-Four

Robin's arrival Saturday morning was like a whirlwind. She flew in through the front door, leaving it ajar as she launched herself into her room, stripping off her clothes as she moved. When she came out ten minutes later, she was dressed in something completely different.

"Uh, where are you going?" Brooke asked, noting the short skirt she had changed into.

"Mr Khan's, I told you, I start work today and..."

"And you need to be wearing something much more appropriate," Brooke stated. She wracked her brain for the tiny piece of memory from when this had been agreed, but as usual, came up lacking.

Robin scoffed. "Oh please. What's wrong with this?"

Brooke raised a brow before turning to Catherine. "Tell her, that is not what a 15-year-old should be wearing to work."

Catherine held her palms up. "Hey, don't get me involved."

Robin stood with her hands on her hips. "See, even Catherine thinks it's okay."

"I didn't say that," Catherine interjected.

"Binnie, go and change," Brooke demanded.

Robin huffed. "You're my sister B, not my mum," she said, flouncing back into her room and slamming the door behind her.

Catherine pursed her lips into a tight understanding smile aimed at Brooke.

"Sorry about that," Brooke offered. "Do you want some tea?"

Catherine was reminded of the morning after their night together. "Actually, I probably should get going. I can give Robin a lift if you like?"

"Oh, yeah of course, thank you."

The door to Robin's room opened and both women turned. The youngster had changed into ripped jeans and shirt. She curtseyed sarcastically. "Happy now?"

"Yes, thank you. Catherine said she can drop you off."

"I'm fine, I can get the bus, *she* should *stay* here with you," she answered quickly, glaring at Catherine.

"I'm fine. Don't even have a headache anymore,"

Deciding that getting out from the middle of this sibling argument was probably the best thing to do, Catherine made her way into Robin's room. Her case was packed; all she had left to do was zip it shut. She looked around the small room and smiled. It had been an experience and she was glad of it. Getting to know Brooke had been fun, but she needed to leave for her own self-preservation. She grabbed her case and went back out.

"Ready to go?" she said brightly.

~FI~

Robin lead the way, her heavy boots clumping down each step. She barely reached the bottom step before she turned back to look at Catherine, who was slowly making her way down. "I can't believe you're skipping out already," Robin said. "This was your chance to work your magic."

Catherine rolled her eyes. Where did this kid her ideas about romance from? "Robin, I've already informed you that Brooke is seeing..."

"Yeah blah blah, I told you there is no way that is a *date* date!" As Catherine reached the bottom step, Robin held the door open for her. "She's mentioned Amber twice, and only to say how much she liked her—"

"See!"

"*As* a colleague to have *lunch* with," she implored, but to no avail. Catherine hit the fob alarm and opened the car door.

"Get in," she sighed.

The car door slammed shut. "I don't get why you're not in there telling her," Robin continued, pulling on the seatbelt.

"Telling her what, Robin? You told me not to tell her!"

"I said she didn't need to find out you was horrible to her, not that you shouldn't ask her out."

Catherine winced. She didn't need to be reminded just how badly she had behaved. "Robin, I'm not..."

"Oh please, Brooke wouldn't let herself fall for someone that hadn't shown any interest, and the fact that you have spent the past 72 hours looking after her, it's pretty clear you care about her too."

Catherine looked ahead at the slow traffic. Roadworks meant temporary lights were in place. "Fine, yes I like her, but it really isn't that simple. I know you want to help, and I know you think a lot of your sister, but the reality is..." She moved the car forward and checked her mirrors before pulling out and taking the next right-hand turn. "The reality is that none of that matters...I can't, okay...so please just let it go. She doesn't remember, so nobody is being hurt anymore."

"I think you're an idiot."

Catherine glanced at her, her brow raised at the insolence. "Thank you."

Chapter Thirty-Five

Amber waited patiently outside of Pollards, rubbing her gloved hands up and down her arms in an effort to keep warm. It was starting to feel a lot more like Christmas in the glow of the window lights, and she was a little excited to be out.

She hadn't been out in weeks, not since her last date with Eric. What a blow-out that had been, too. So, she was due some fun, and Brooke seemed like just the person to spend her free time with until she worked up the nerve to approach Brian.

They'd spent the better part of the morning texting plans for the evening ahead, and she was looking forward to it. Brooke was a new friend, sure, but she hadn't seen her since the injury, and there wasn't too much information about that, so she was really interested in catching up with her.

She had left it up to Brooke to decide where they were going. Her only instructions were that it had to be fun and something they dressed up for, which explained why she was so cold now in a flimsy jacket, short skirt, and heels.

Looking up from her phone, she realised Brooke was there, standing by the entrance looking lost. Her eyes scanned the area twice, looking past Amber.

Amber laughed. "Hey, forgotten what I look like already?" she called out as she walked towards her. She had scrubbed up well, like Amber knew she would.

"Amber?" Brooke stuttered. She tried to take in as much detail about the approaching woman as she could, hoping that something would trigger a memory, but so far, no.

"Of course, who else was you expecting?"

Brooke smiled, a little nervously. "I uh...nobody of course, I hope you wasn't waiting long?"

Amber kissed her cheek in greeting and then linked arms with her. "Nope, just got here really. So, where are you taking me?"

Brooke quickly put the clues together. The texts. The kiss to the cheek, linking arms...this *was* a date. She contemplated for a moment whether to be upfront about not remembering her, but then, what did it matter? Here she was, on a Saturday night, out with an attractive woman. Albeit not her usual type. Why not just enjoy it?

They walked along the high street. It was getting windy, and Amber gripped her arm a little more tightly, pulling them closer together. "So, I remember reading about this place, uh a bar...it's called Art..." Brooke said.

"Oh, yes, I have read about it!" Amber exclaimed, excitedly stopping in her tracks. "I was reading about the owner; did you know she worked at Pollards? Just before I started, in fact. I think I got her job."

"Really, wow that is something," Brooke said as they walked on.

"Yeah, she married an actress. So, this bar is a gay bar, right?"

"Um yeah, I guess, I've never been, so I don't know what it's like really."

~FI~

There was a small queue already forming to get inside Art. Amber and Brooke joined the end of it, and by the time they were at the door waiting to be let in, Brooke had discovered quite a lot about Amber and pretty much understood why she liked her.

"Hey, good to see you again," the woman on the door said as she held it open for them. Brooke nodded out of politeness and followed Amber inside.

"I thought you said you haven't been here before?"

Shrugging her coat off, Brooke replied, "I haven't, she must have me mistaken for someone else. What would you like to drink?" she asked, a little louder as the music began to get livelier the further into the bar they ventured.

"Oh, anything with vodka," Amber replied, grinning at her. "I'll go grab us some seats, okay?" she said, pointing to a table in the corner that was about to become free. Brooke nodded and turned back to the bar to wait for a member of the bar team to notice her. The club was busy. Brooke scanned the room while she waited; it looked like a nice place at least. She ordered their drinks and was just handing over the cash to pay when she noticed someone out of the periphery of her vision. Catherine.

She was stunning, that was the first thing that Brooke noticed. Nothing like the casual Catherine who had been staying with her for the past 72 hours. She wasn't alone, either. A darker-haired woman was leaning into her space, speaking into her ear. Whatever she said had made Catherine laugh. Brooke was entranced just watching her. The woman with her was now smiling, her full attention on Catherine as she spoke and then, just as the girl behind the bar returned with her change, the woman leaned in and kissed Catherine. The kind of kiss only lovers shared. Feeling as though she were prying, she turned away quickly.

Drinks in hand, she made her way through the throng of people to where Amber was sitting, looking around the room.

"This place is great. I am glad you asked me to join you," Amber said.

"I am surprised you haven't been asked by anyone else," Brooke said, turning to face her.

"Why would I have been here before?"

Brooke shrugged and took a sip of her drink. "I dunno, I just assumed, you know, an attractive woman like you would have the ladies beating down the door to take her somewhere like this."

"Ladies?" Amber laughed, a little confused by Brooke's assumption. Hadn't she told her about Eric and Brian? "I'm not gay."

Brooke coughed. "You're not?" This was the most confusing and bizarre date she had ever been on.

Amber shook her head, pink hair flying left, then right. "No, not that I'm not up for a little fun now and then." She winked before leaning in to speak against Brooke's ear. "Okay I'll be honest, the idea of kissing a woman is pretty hot, but I haven't."

"You haven't?"

"Not yet." Blue eyes scanned Brooke's face, deciding something. "I'd kiss you though." She giggled and sucked her drink through the straw.

Brooke blushed and glanced away, back across the room. Catherine was still there, pressed up against her date now. Something about the image caused a flood of...anger? No, jealousy, to flush through her thoughts, which was crazy. Catherine was entitled to see whomever she liked; she had just never assumed that it would be a woman. She hadn't noticed Amber slide closer to her until she felt their thighs touch. Making up her mind, she turned back to Amber and found herself nose to nose. Without further thought, Brooke tilted her head and kissed her.

"Okay?" she asked as the kiss ended. Amber was looking at her a little dazed, as though Brooke was the most exciting person alive.

"Yeah, I wasn't expecting it to be *that* good," she said, laughing as she now composed herself and sipped some more of her drink.

"Well, I figured there was only one way to make sure you knew if you wanted the date to continue." Brooke laughed too.

"Date?" she said, leaning in and initiating the next kiss.

Brooke didn't disappoint. "This isn't a date?" she asked, flummoxed by the night's events so far.

"Well, it wasn't, but...Brooke, are you okay? Did that bang on the head do something?" Amber was amused.

"Okay, so I kind of do have a little memory loss, and when you texted asking about tonight, I just assumed it was a date and that it would be really rude to tell you that I had no idea who you were." She winced a little at the admission. "I thought once I met you that maybe I'd remember..."

Amber burst out laughing. "Oh Brooke, that is just classic." She leaned forward and kissed her again. "Alright, so we hit it off at work and I'll be honest, you kind of intrigue me a little. You got this whole sexy confident thing going on and that's attractive, even to me. But ultimately, I'm into guys."

Brooke nodded. "Okay, I think that might be the nicest brush off."

"Oh, I'm not brushing you off. Tonight, is what it is, two friends having fun." She winked again. "If you're interested in a friends with benefits kind of thing for the night?"

"We need more drinks," Brooke said, rising from her seat. "Same again?"

Amber nodded and pulled her back down to her for one more kiss. "No strings, Brooke." When Brooke looked-up she saw Catherine staring right at her from across the dance floor. Just for a second, she had a moment of déjà vu, a fleeting flash of something she couldn't quite grasp. Brooke smiled at Amber as she picked up their empty glasses and walked up to the bar. She tried not to look over at Catherine. The woman deserved her privacy, but it was difficult. Her subconscious kept dragging her line of sight in that direction.

Catherine caught Brooke staring again and smiled. Her companion glanced over and scowled, sliding an arm around Catherine's waist possessively.

"What can I get ya?" shouted the same girl over the bar.

Brooke turned her attention away from the two women and back to the drinks order. "One vodka and lemonade and a Coke, please."

Something about Catherine in this environment stood out to Brooke. She searched her memory banks and desperately delved deeper to unlock the answer. She didn't have it; just a bunch of assumptions and maybes. She thought back to the woman on the door recognising her. Maybe she *had* been in here before. If she had, and Catherine had been in here, then she most likely would have noticed her. It wasn't that big a place after all, and someone like Catherine stood out.

Shaking her head, she put those thoughts out of her mind. The drinks were cold in her hands as she turned and headed back to her seat. Amber was moving to the music and when her eyes fell on Brooke, she beamed at her. She was definitely cute, Brooke thought.

"You were gone far too long," Amber complained playfully, kissing Brooke the moment she sat back down.

Brooke grinned. "For someone that has never dated a woman, you sure have taken to kissing one."

"Well you're such a good kisser," she replied grinning as she sipped her drink, the alcohol starting to go to her head a little.

"Yeah? That's not all I am good at." Brooke winked with growing confidence. A night of fun with Amber was looking more and more interesting.

"Oh, don't worry, I am planning to find out," she said as she licked her lip before biting down gently on it. "Dance with me?" she said, suddenly standing and making a grab for Brooke's hand. Brooke swallowed down her drink in one. She wasn't that much of a dancer usually, but what the hell. Amber was short, but what she lacked in height, she made up for in dance moves. Her arms slid easily around Brooke's neck as she brought their bodies closer together and let the beat dictate the sway of her hips and the push of her pelvis. Clearly, she was an expert in dancing dirty. Heat built between them; this night was definitely heading to an explosive ending. After several songs, Brooke grinned. "I need a break," she said, pointing over her shoulder towards the toilets.

"Another round?" Amber asked, already turning towards the bar.

~FI~

As with most bars nowadays, a lack of cubicles meant a queue. Brooke joined the back of it and waited her turn. There were friendly smiles and nods of acknowledgement as women leaving passed those queueing. Looking down the line, she could see Catherine at the front. She was about to call out when a tall woman in a suit stepped out and held the door for Catherine. Luckily for Brooke, the other three cubicles must have vacated at the same time because the queue suddenly moved forward quickly, and Brooke was able to take the end one.

When she came out, she found Catherine at the sink applying lipstick. Their eyes locked through the mirror.

"Having fun, I see?" Catherine said it with a smile, but Brooke could definitely detect an undercurrent of something else there. She just couldn't work out what it was.

"Yes, we're having a great time, you too by the look of it." She heard the slight tremor of her own voice and recognised that small thump of jealousy again.

"Hmm well, needs must," Catherine mumbled as she turned back around to face the mirror, checking her lipstick once more. Brooke narrowed her eyes, unsure what that meant. "So, Amber? All good now that you've been...reacquainted?" She looked away once she had finished the question.

"Yeah, she's uh...fun." Brooke smiled. Reaching up, she rubbed her head where the stitches were. Catherine didn't reply. Instead she just smiled and looked at her through the mirror, again re-checking her lipstick.

"I'd prefer if my...." she said, turning back to Brooke and moving closer. "...private life remained so..." Their eyes locked onto one another. Catherine was barely a foot away. She placed her palms flat upon Brooke's upper chest and let her gaze briefly drop to her mouth. "I'll see you at work on Monday," she said, smoothing the material of her shirt before walking out of the restroom.

It was only then that Brooke realised she had been holding her breath.

Chapter Thirty-Six

Brooke didn't know what she wanted, and for that reason alone, she didn't take things any further with Amber. They spent the rest of the night dancing, even kissing, but that was it. Amber had been more fun than she had ever expected from an anonymous date, but it was a no-go for so many reasons.

She did know, however, that she was very attracted to Catherine, and from what she remembered of their conversation in the bathroom, she had a feeling Catherine might feel the same way. But there was something that nagged at her and told her not to go there, and she didn't quite understand why, because they had gotten on so well that – well, it would be easy to see Catherine as someone more...important?

Amber met her downstairs. She wore her uniform and carried 4 cups of coffee in a take-out tray and a bag of pastries. Every now and then they passed a room and Brooke was sure she knew it, but then Amber would reel off the department name and Brooke would just shake her head in frustration. She concentrated hard on trying to remember the way, but it was a maze.

"Well, here we are. Human Resources Department," Amber announced from outside the door. "Now, I know you said that Ms Blake...I mean, Catherine, is this nice woman and that she looked after you. I still can't believe she did that though, but Brooke, I have to tell you that *that* Catherine...she doesn't..."

Catherine was already in her office when Brooke strolled right up to the door, knocking without a thought.

"Brooke, I wouldn't—" Amber was saying, but it was too late. She'd already opened the door.

"I don't know about you, but I need this," Brooke said, grinning as she waltzed in. She smiled brightly at Catherine, expecting a happy face in return. The look of anger that masked Catherine's features was quickly replaced with confusion, but both threw Brooke.

"I...uh." The old Catherine still very much thought to react with disdain. She froze, not quite sure how to answer. Not to mention that the uniform was very distracting.

"Sorry, were you busy? I should have waited, right? I just thought..." She held the two cups of coffee as evidence. "I'll just..." She placed one cup down on the desk and began to retreat.

Finally, Catherine got herself together. "I feel quite refreshed, actually." She tried a smile and picked up the cup of coffee. "So, good weekend I take it?" she asked, the smile a little brighter on her face now, but the tone a little subdued.

"The best," Brooke said, grinning once more. "I really needed that, sometimes you just have to let loose. Know what I mean?" she asked as she opened the bag and pulled a pain au chocolat out before passing the bag back across to Catherine.

"Yes, I think it is prudent to let one's hair down occasionally," Catherine said, and Brooke couldn't help but notice the difference in 'office' Catherine to 'out of office' Catherine.

"You seemed to be having fun with your *friend.*"

"I was, yes," Catherine said, declining the pastries and picking up her pile of files, moving them from one pile to another.

"I didn't think you were seeing anyone?" Brooke said. She wanted to take a seat, but had the impression that she wouldn't be welcome to. Was Catherine nervous about something?

"Sorry, what?" Catherine asked, her attention firmly on the file in hand.

"I said." She was enjoying this for some reason. "I thought you were single?"

"Oh," Catherine replied and finally looked up at Brooke. "Yes." Now that was an answer Brooke hadn't expected. "Uh, well it's...Petra is just..."

"Friends with benefits cos you can't be with the one you really like?"

Catherine sighed. She was starting to feel uncomfortable. "I don't think it is really an appropriate work discussion. If you don't mind, I have work to do." And just like that, the shutters were up.

"Right, so what do you want me to do while I am here?"

Catherine chastised herself. The time spent with Brooke had been eye-opening. She wanted to try and be a little more open and friendlier at work. She had taken on this persona in order to avoid being the workplace gossip, and instead had still become the person they all talked about behind her back, just for different reasons. She wanted to change that, but knowing how to do it was not something she had worked out yet.

"You can sit here and help me with these files if you like?"

Brooke looked at the pile of files and frowned. "You don't want me to start with my training?"

"Well, if you want to go and sit with Amber and do that then that's fine, I just thought..." What did she think? *That if you stayed in here with me, you'd realise how much you used to like me and maybe you'll forget all about Amber instead?* "If you just got into the swing of things, maybe your memory will come back and you won't need to redo all the SOPs." She mentally high-fived herself for coming up with that. "Oh, and there's no need to wear the uniform while you're in the office."

"Alright." Brooke pulled over the swivel chair from the corner and sat herself down on the opposite side of the desk to Catherine. The blonde smiled and pushed the pile of files into the middle of the desk.

"Each file needs to be organised into the right order internally, and then all the files need to be placed in alphabetical order back into the cabinet in the other office." She pulled a sheet of paper from her drawer and handed it to Brooke. "That's the list order for each file."

"Okay, sounds simple enough."

A comfortable silence existed between them as they worked on their own. It wasn't long, however, before Brooke began to fidget. These files were boring.

Brooke and boring didn't mix well.

"You should take a break, Brooke," Catherine said without looking up from her computer.

Brooke stared at her. "I'm okay, thanks Catherine." It might be boring work, but she was determined to get it done.

Catherine sat back in her chair, pushed her glasses back up her nose, and observed her. "It wasn't a choice, Brooke. I am to make sure you take a break every couple of hours."

Brooke checked her watch; almost 11 a.m. "Oh, right. I'll go get some coffee. Would you like one?" she asked, rising from her chair.

"Yes, thank you, that would be nice." She reached down and into her bag. Pulling her purse from it, she opened it and took out a £20 note. "Please get something for Kim and Amber too. And make sure you take the full fifteen minutes."

"What if I got some lunch but ate it here and we got to know each other some more?" Brooke asked, sitting back in her chair and spinning around.

"Why would we do that?" Catherine asked, frowning at her antics. She might be trying to be a little warmer, but this was still the workplace.

"Cos it's fun?" Brooke grinned, spinning again.

"Is it?" Catherine replied, watching her closely now and considering whether she should insist she stop spinning on the chair.

"You don't think so?"

"I think that you need to take a break away from the office, and I need a break from you and your spinning."

Catherine smirked at her, and it looked more familiar than any other time. She sighed when the memory wouldn't come. "Does anyone here know anything about you, Catherine?" When the older woman remained quiet, Brooke tried again. "It's just...I think you're great, you know? I just wanted you to know that."

"Thank you, that's...I appreciate that. Now, you still need to take a break."

"Okay, but I will be back," she said, standing to leave again. "And spinning is fun, you should try it," she added over her shoulder as she left the room.

Catherine shook her head and smiled to herself. *Spinning?* She suddenly felt silly when the thought popped into her head. Looking up to check nobody could see, she spun in her chair. Feeling instantly giddy, she grabbed hold of the edge of the desk to stop herself and laughed.

Brooke was right; it was fun.

Chapter Thirty-Seven

Catherine wore her hair up, and Brooke found herself mesmerised by the join of her neck and shoulder. She was due another break, but had been deliberately keeping quiet, hoping that Catherine wouldn't notice and she could just sit here and continue staring at her while she pretended to peruse a file. Which was fine, because she had already sorted it into order.

She had been noticing things like that a lot over the last couple of days. Mainly she had put it down to two things. One, she had spent a lot of time with Catherine recently, so it was obvious that she was going to notice things about her, but two, she had realised that she was more than attracted to her. Every time Catherine looked over at her and pushed those glasses back into place, it sent a little thrill through Brooke.

For almost 40 minutes, Catherine had been busy with her emails and had barely spoken. Brooke wondered if she knew just how adorable she was when she chewed on a pen and thought too hard. The tip of her tongue would poke out between her lips and would leave Brooke wondering what it would feel like to have that tongue explore parts of her body in such an attentive way.

"It's 10.43, Brooke. Shouldn't you have gone on a break by now?" Catherine asked without looking up.

Brooke sighed, audibly. "I just have these last..."

"You're bored. You've been reading that same file for 8 minutes now," she said, finally looking up and straight at Brooke. "Take a break." An email pinged and took her attention back to work.

Brooke put the file on the finished pile. "Why don't you join me?"

"I'd love to," she said. "However, I have 43 emails to read. Why don't you ask Amber?"

Brooke stood up and pushed her chair in. "Okay." She lingered in place a moment longer until Catherine looked up again. There was a heavy moment of something unspoken between them. "I'll bring you some tea back then?"

"That would be nice, thank you."

"Alright then." She smiled. Brooke didn't seem to want to leave. "Are you sure you don't want to?" She pointed her thumb over her shoulder towards the canteen.

God, yes. All I want to do is join you, but you have Amber. "Another time, maybe."

~Fl~

Each break she took, Brooke would invite Catherine to join her, and each time, Catherine would politely decline. It confused Brooke no end. She thought they were friends and that as such, they should spend time together, but since being back to work, Catherine had almost put an invisible block up between them.

The end of the week came rapidly, and by Friday both Catherine and Brooke had pretty much managed to get through everything Catherine needed doing. Still her memory hadn't returned.

Over the week, the office had become a lot more relaxed where Catherine was concerned. Kim and Amber had both noticed the change in their boss, but neither had voiced it any louder than a raise of a brow or a grin at each other across the desks. They didn't want to jinx it. Catherine's office door had even remained open most of the time. There was an easier, more natural back-and-forth between the two offices and it was clear that it had something to do with Brooke.

Catherine had some emails she was going through and Brooke was finishing organising the last few files when Amber popped her head around the door.

"Hey you, I am nearly finished. Do you wanna grab a beer and something to eat later?" Amber said to Brooke. Catherine didn't look up.

"Yes! That would be great. Robin is out with friends. We should be done here in 30 minutes. Do you want me to meet you there?" Brooke replied, glancing at Catherine as she spoke. Catherine still hadn't moved, like literally hadn't moved. She was as still as a statue, and it intrigued Brooke. "Would you like to join us, Catherine?"

She watched as Catherine swallowed before she slowly looked up from her screen, first at Amber and then at Brooke.

"Oh, thank you, but no, I have somewhere else I need to be." And that somewhere else was anywhere she didn't have to watch Brooke canoodling with Amber. She wished Brooke happiness, but that didn't mean she had to endure watching it play out in front of her.

Brooke shrugged and turned her attention back to Amber. "So, I'll meet you in Roosters then? Get a good table and have my beer waiting, woman!" she called out, smiling. As Amber turned to leave, she gave Brooke the finger.

"You two seem to have hit it off," Catherine said, continuing to type her reply to the email she had just read.

"Yeah, Amber is really cool. I like hanging out with her. We have a lot of fun," Brooke answered honestly, because it was true. They had lunch together most days, and Brooke was enjoying having a girl for a friend. In the army most of her colleagues were men, which was fine, but there were times when all she wanted was another female to bitch about periods and girl stuff.

"Oh, not now," Catherine said, suddenly flinging her pen on her desk in annoyance. She sat back in her chair and took a deep and frustrated breath.

"Sorry?"

"Oh Brooke, not you. I just received an email from head office. We have an audit to do due to some discrepancies at several other branches."

"Oh ok, what does that mean?"

"It means that by the end of next week I have to go through every file, and make sure every I is dotted, every T is crossed, because someone, somewhere, cocked something up, and there will be another someone coming down from Manchester to go through it all, and not just in this department, but in every department, and I just don't know how they expect me to have everything organised in a week!" She leant forward, elbows resting on the table as she propped her head up in her palms.

"Alright, breathe!" Brooke was concerned that Catherine might combust. "I can help," she said, hesitantly. "If that would be okay?" Amber and Kim were already busy; an extra pair of hands would surely help spread the load, and it wasn't like she had anything better to do right now.

Catherine looked up. Brooke, sitting opposite her with a crooked smile on her face, looking all cute and wonderful. She felt like crying. She closed her eyes and composed herself with several deep breaths.

"Thank you, yes that would help greatly." Her voice was breathy and stuttering. Brooke frowned in frustration for her.

"Okay then, so it's Friday and we're almost done. There is no point sitting here all night worrying about it. Go and enjoy the weekend, and Monday we will get stuck in. Those auditors will be amazed at how brilliant you are."

Catherine smiled at the compliment. "You really are special. Have a great time with Amber," she offered sincerely.

~Fl~

Amber had a beer waiting and menus ready to order. Roosters was a typical bar eatery. It served chicken mainly – the clue was in the name of the place after all – but it was clean and friendly, and they had a great seat away from the door that chucked a bucket of cold over anyone in its vicinity every time someone new entered.

"I thought you had forgotten me!" Amber complained half-heartedly as Brooke slid into the booth opposite her.

"Never. How could that ever happen? Nobody body-slammed me today!" Brooke grinned at her own joke. "I was just talking to Catherine, that's all."

"Oh yes, Catherine." Amber winked.

Brooke tilted her head quizzically. "What is that supposed to mean?" She took a quick swig of her beer.

Leaning across the table, Amber whispered, "You want to fuck her?"

Brooke almost choked on her beer as she spluttered and coughed, causing Amber to burst out laughing.

"Seriously, Amber!"

"What? It is true, I see the way you look at her," she said, leaning forward and sucking on her straw.

"And just how do I look at her?"

"Like you want to fuck her!" As Amber said the words, an image flashed into Brooke's mind of Catherine at her desk, her blouse unbuttoned two buttons more than they needed to be.

"I will admit she is very attractive," Brooke agreed, taking another sip of her beer.

"Attractive? She is downright hot. She could have been on the cover of a magazine and not look out of place," Amber continued. "I mean I get it, jeez, even I would." She laughed.

"Well, feel free to take a shot," Brooke threw back as she picked up the menu and perused it, hoping that Amber would change the subject. She couldn't fathom why she was so uncomfortable talking about Catherine like that. Amber was right; she did want to go to bed with Catherine. Maybe that was the problem: Brooke didn't view Catherine as just a fuck. Catherine was classy. She deserved wooing properly and being taken to nice restaurants.

"And step on your toes? No chance! Anyway, she likes you too."

"What? Since when have you become the lesbian love guru of England?" Brooke laughed once more. "I am having the chicken."

"Well of course you are, what else is there to have?" Amber agreed as she too checked out the menu for the third time. "I have watched the two of you all week. She thinks we are shagging, and she hates me for it."

"No, I told her we're just have fun hanging out."

"I'm telling you, she thinks we are sleeping together." She watched as Brooke frowned. "I tell ya what? On Monday I will come to the office and flirt with you. Flirt back, watch her reaction." She sipped her drink. "She. Likes. You!"

~FI~

The weekend for Catherine was a last-minute attempt to find some form of relaxation. She even had her hair cut.

Everything at work was up in the air because of the urgent audit she faced and yet, she still couldn't get Brooke out of her mind. The idea that she was spending the weekend with Amber again just filled her with sadness.

She kept herself busy and tried desperately to keep her thoughts away from what she thought Brooke and Amber must surely be getting up to, but she failed and spent long moments envious of Amber. Amber was at least fifteen years her junior; eager, fun, and attractive. Amber was everything Catherine felt she wasn't.

Those few moments spent in the arms of Brooke Chambers had been the most exciting she had spent with another person while naked in a very long time.

If she concentrated hard enough, she could still feel the heat from Brooke's fingers as they torturously searched and mapped her skin, and the taste of her lips and tongue as she invaded her mouth and made her knees go weak.

"Jesus," she muttered to herself.

Chapter Thirty-Eight

On Monday morning, Catherine was at work early as usual. She had every file listed and organised in order for checking and rechecking – every training record, every uniform order form. If HR dealt with it, then she would have it covered, and with help from Brooke and her team, they would find any discrepancies and fix them before Mr. Foxworth arrived on Friday to go through them.

And just as though by thinking about her she had conjured her up, there she stood in the doorway watching her. Once again, she carried coffee and a bag of pastries. She wore jeans today that hung low on her hips, the shallow dips there just visible when she lifted her hand to show Catherine the pastries and her button-down fitted plaid shirt rose up slightly. Catherine felt her mouth dry and she swallowed, unable to speak, so she just smiled.

"I figured you would be here early, so..." Brooke gave a 'here I am too' shrug and stepped into the office. She set the coffee down next to the pastries before just ripping the bag open to reveal two pain au chocolat'. Catherine's favourite.

"I didn't expect you to come in early too, Brooke," she said, once she could finally find her voice.

"More hands on deck, the quicker we get finished, and the quicker we can go for a drink!" Brooke said, watching Catherine's reaction.

"I am sure Amber will be only too pleased to have you finished early," Catherine replied, and there it was, that undertone of something Brooke could never quite put her finger on until now. Was Amber correct? Was it really jealousy?

"Oh, Amber won't mind you and I going for a drink. In fact, she suggested it."

Catherine didn't reply right away. Instead she stood and went to a file drawer. Opening it, she said, "I think we will start here. If we take half the files each, then we can quickly get through each drawer and mark off the areas that we have finished."

"Alright, and then we can go for a drink?" Brooke said. She was smiling and not prepared to back down.

"Why?" Catherine asked, looking at her seriously. Brooke was just relentless about it. If it was one thing Catherine couldn't take, it was being the butt of somebody else's joke, and that's what this was starting to feel like.

"What do you mean, why? Isn't it customary for friends to hang out?" Brooke said, picking up a pastry and pulling a piece off.

Catherine's gaze followed the morsel as it was placed between open lips. She remembered those lips encased around her own nipple, warm and wet as they tugged...she shook herself back into reality. "I guess so, however I don't understand why Amber suggested it?"

"Um, because she thinks we would have fun?" Brooke said honestly, although she left the part out where Amber suggested *how* they would have fun.

"Well, let's just get on and see how we do before we get ahead of ourselves and think about fun," Catherine said abruptly, handing the files to Brooke. Before seating herself at her own side of the desk with her half of the remaining files, she cast a glance out of the window. The sky a shadowy grey between white clouds that drifted with the wind. Sometimes she felt as though she were just a cloud, being blown through life. Maybe she did need some fun.

"By the way, I like your new hairstyle," Brooke said, gaining her attention. She grinned across the desk as she stuffed the last piece of pain au Chocolat into her mouth.

Catherine turned away again, smiling that Brooke had noticed.

Chapter Thirty-Nine

The café was quite busy by the time Brooke's lunch break came around, filling up with customers taking a break from Christmas shopping. She lined up in the queue and pushed her tray along with them.

Amber was going to meet her as soon as she was done with her paperwork. So, for now she could just sit back and people watch for a minute or two.

Grabbing a pre-made sandwich and a bottle of water, she paid and then found some seats that overlooked the shop floor. It all felt somewhat familiar to her; of course, she had used Pollards to shop long before hitting her head. Her parents had always lived in the area, and Pollards was the biggest store in town, so everyone knew it. The store looked very Christmassy with all the lights flashing and the decorations sparking. She hummed along to *Rudolph the Red-Nosed Reindeer* as it played out of the store sound system. Adverts popped up every now and then, informing customers of great deals they just had to buy. Someone had left a copy of today's newspaper, and she scanned the front page: another celebrity caught with their pants down.

"Yo, Chambers. You're back!" exclaimed a loud voice from behind her. She turned to find a tall man in uniform grinning at her.

"Uh, yeah...sorry." She glanced down at his name badge. S Potter...she had no clue who he was or what the S stood for. "Lost some memory from the bang on the head."

Forget it

Without invitation, he sat down on the seat opposite. "That's what I heard. Almighty thump then. Good job I was there to help."

"Well, thanks." She grinned.

"So, when are you back out there with me?" he asked, his chin jutting towards the store.

"I'm not sure. I have to redo all of my training and get a doctor's approval. Till then I am stuck in the HR office."

He sucked in a breath. "With the ice queen? As if getting your head caved in wasn't enough." He chuckled.

"Catherine? She's okay."

"Don't let her catch you calling her Catherine. *It's Ms Blake,*" he said, imitating her. "Anyway, I thought you and her had issues?"

"What kind of issues?" She was genuinely confused about the question. Catherine was a friend; why would they have issues?

He shrugged and stood. "Dunno, I just got the impression she didn't like you, and you weren't that enamoured with her either. Anyway, best get back to it. Good to see you back."

He walked off, leaving Brooke with more questions than she started with. By the time Amber appeared, she was bouncing her knee with apprehension.

"What's up with you?" Amber asked, flopping down into the seat Potter had vacated. "You're like a coiled spring waiting to ping."

Brooke rubbed her face, her hand reaching around to touch the small covering over her stitches. "Nothing," she said too quickly.

Amber cocked a brow and pursed her lips. "Right, and I'm the queen. Spill it," she demanded, picking up the uneaten half of Brooke's sandwich and taking a bite.

"Do I...did I, I mean before I hit my head and forgot everything...did I like Catherine?"

Amber sat back in her chair, one side of her mouth twitched upwards. "Well, honestly I don't know." Brooke frowned. That wasn't the helpful answer she wanted. "Ms Blake isn't...until now, she hasn't been the easiest person to get along with. She's polite and very good at her job, but she's not very...sociable. All I can tell you is that you started working here and she was her usual forthright self. But even when Kim and I explained what she was like, you seemed intent on trying to be nice to her."

"In what way?"

Amber took another bite of the sandwich. When she finished chewing, she explained, "Well for instance, you would come into the office with coffee and tea for us all, including Catherine."

"Right, well that's just...I did that this morning and she..."

Amber cut her off. "I know, but back then she didn't like it. Something is different with her lately though, and I think that stems from you."

"I just don't get it. Why would she be mad at me for bringing her a hot drink?" That just sounded preposterous.

"Well, all I can tell you is that one morning she stormed into the office and demanded to see you. I've never seen her that angry," she added, "When you arrived, she made me and Kim leave the office. It's not hard to hear a raised voice in this place, even from the hallway. It was muffled, but she was definitely ripping you a new one."

Brooke screwed up her face. "This is so frustrating!" She stood up abruptly.

"Brooke? Wait..."

"I'll be fine, I just...I need some space," she called over her shoulder as she all but ran from the restaurant.

Chapter Forty

Brooke was frozen. The quick walk around the block, though, had helped. Every step had loosened something else at the back of her consciousness. Amber and Potter's words mixed her up and tossed her thoughts around, but in the end, they seemed to settle and make sense. Something clicked, and images began to pop in and out of her mind's eye so fast that she could barely keep up, but now as she stood outside of Catherine's office, rapidly running her palms up and down her arms in an effort to warm up, she knew what she had forgotten: Catherine.

There were a lot more questions than answers, and she had a lot of things to discuss with Robin too, but right now there was only one thing she wanted to find out.

Taking the bull by the horns, she grasped the handle to Catherine's door and pushed it open without knocking.

The object of all her attention was on the phone. She looked up, frowning, and for a moment Brooke considered backing out, but she had come this far and right now, some things were more important than Catherine having a bee in her bonnet about work. She ignored the glare, closed the door behind her, sat down in the chair opposite Catherine, and waited.

"Roger, I am going to have to call you back, something...important has come up," she said into the handset. "Yes, yes, okay, that will be fine. Thank you." Slowly she brought the handset from her ear and placed it back in its cradle, her eyes set on Brooke the entire time. She felt a little unnerved as the security guard seemed to have zoned out as she continued to just stare at her. "You do realise that its polite to knock on a closed door before you barge in?" Catherine said when nothing was forthcoming from Brooke.

Brooke nodded. "I do, yes."

"Right, well in future, please..."

Brooke interrupted her, grinning. "I'm not sleeping with Amber."

"I really don't need a rundown of your love life, Brooke," Catherine said. She looked away at her computer just to avoid that penetrating stare. When Brooke laughed, her attention was brought back to the brunette. "Brooke, are you okay? Is it your head?" She grew concerned now at the strange behaviour.

"Yes, it's my head," Brooke confirmed, nodding now along with the grinning. "Do you want to go for a drink?"

"As I have said before..."

"I was thinking Art, or maybe we could head down to Brighton and I could win you a matching Penguin? I'm really good at those shoot 'em up games."

Catherine felt the air leave her lungs. "What?"

Brooke leant across the desk and lowered her voice. "Or...we could just spend the weekend in bed again."

The palm of Catherine's right hand flew to her chest. "You remember?"

Brooke nodded. "Not everything, things are still dropping into place and I'm trying to make sense of a lot of stuff, but yes, Catherine...I remember you."

The air in the room stilled. Catherine's skin flushed and heated as she tried to fathom what this all now meant.

"I can explain," she began. The phone on her desk began to ring, but she ignored it. "The thing is..."

"You made a mistake?"

Catherine nodded.

"All I want to know is which part was the mistake? Ending things when you did and being mean in order to make me leave you alone, or coming to stay and look after me, letting me start to like you all over again?"

"First bit," Catherine said quickly, unsure where Brooke was taking this. "I shouldn't have." She swallowed and took a deep breath. "I wish I hadn't done that."

Brooke nodded and let those words settle. "So, if we drew a line in the sand..." She was interrupted by the phone ringing again, and she followed Catherine's gaze towards it. "Answer it."

Catherine shook her head. "No, I want..." She stood up and came around the desk, grabbing her coat from its hook on the wall. "Come on, we can't talk here."

~FI~

The 20-minute drive had been relatively silent. Catherine had asked when her memory had returned, and Brooke had filled her in on the conversations she had had with Amber over the last few days and the brisk walk that had helped nudge things along.

When she mentioned that Amber thought she was jealous and had assumed they were sleeping together, Catherine felt the heat rise in her cheeks. Amber was a smart girl.

"Amber thinks that I...does she know? About us? Did you tell her?"

"Of course not, she just said it was obvious just by looking at us that we both had the hots for each other." Brooke glanced out of the window and didn't recognise the street they were on. "Where are we going?"

"My house. It's quiet there, no interruptions. I want this sorted one way or the other," Catherine stated as she pulled into the drive of a small two-storey detached house. Switching the engine off, she turned to face Brooke, and the younger woman was instantly reminded of the night they had last seen each other, when Catherine had been smiling at her and making a move. "Are you coming in?" she asked, when Brooke made no move to release the seatbelt.

"Yeah."

Catherine's house was warm as they entered together. Not just physically, but aesthetically too. Warm browns and reds adorned the walls and furnishings. Soft lighting lit the walls and the artwork that adorned it. It was fresh and modern, but homely; a lot like Catherine.

"Tea?" Catherine asked as she placed her bag on the floor by the door and hung up her coat. Brooke nodded and kicked off her shoes when Catherine did, following along behind her towards the kitchen.

Fresh white walls and shiny cupboards glimmered in the late afternoon sunlight that filtered in through the large window. It looked out to the small but perfectly tidy garden, a small lawn with manicured beds of deadheaded flowers and bushes that were still holding their own despite the cold of winter seeping in to stifle them.

A small breakfast bar with two stools separated the space, and Brooke pulled a stool out, sliding onto it easily as Catherine filled the kettle.

"I need to know something, before we do this..." Catherine said. Her back still to Brooke, she stared out into the garden at a small chaffinch that had flown down and landed in the bare branches of the apple tree.

"What's that?"

She turned to face Brooke, licking her bottom lip as she thought for the words. "I want so much to trust you..." She looked away again, fighting the urge to cry. "I just..."

Brooke stood up and rounded the bar. Standing in front of Catherine, she reached out a shaky hand. Her fingertip gently connected to Catherine's chin and lifted. "There is only one way to find out, and that's to let me show you. But I can't do that if you keep these walls up."

Catherine stared into those dark eyes and searched them for any ounce of insincerity and found none. Brooke's palm cupped her cheek and she fell into its warmth, wanting so badly to feel her touch. She closed her eyes, and when Brooke's lips touched her own, she succumbed easily to the kiss. Falling into it, her lips yielded to Brooke's gentle assault on her mouth.

"Wait," she whispered as she broke away. "Wait, we should talk about..."

"Yes, we should, but don't wanna," Brooke argued before pulling at Catherine's waist and tugging her impossibly tighter as she pressed her lips against the blonde's mouth once again. Her tongue was hot and soft as it slid inside and took control of the tempo. Brooke's hands were already under Catherine's blouse. "Tell me you want this?" Brooke whispered against swollen lips.

"I do...but..." She hadn't ever been this turned on with any other person, but Catherine was a pragmatic woman, and this needed to stop. They needed to talk. With all her willpower, she pushed Brooke away, groaning in wanton need as she did so. "Talking   first,"   she   said,   panting   for   breath.

Chapter Forty-One

The point of talking was that one person had to start, and as Catherine poured the tea from the pot and concentrated on adding milk to the cups, Brooke considered what it was she wanted to know, but Catherine beat her to it.

"I want to tell you about Penny," Catherine announced, placing the pot down on the coaster with a small donk sound. In hindsight, this was what she should have done instead of panicking and ending potentially the best opportunity for a relationship she'd had in a long time. "In my last employment I'd worked my way from the entry level position to assistant HR manager. I'd worked there for years and had built a solid reputation. I am good at my job, but affairs of the heart..." She sighed and looked away, gathering her thoughts. "I met Penny at work and things instantly became *intense*." She chanced a glance at Brooke. She had her head propped up in her hands, just as intensely following the story. "We had quite a volatile relationship. Penny was..." She considered how best to describe her ex. "A little passionate in everything she did, and that included me. She wanted the world to know every detail of our life, and I didn't. While things were good between us, she respected that privacy, but then things changed and..." She swallowed, her breath shuddering as she exhaled. This was a lot harder than she had thought it would be. It was dredging up old painful memories, but she pushed on. Brooke deserved the truth. "Eventually, we broke up...I thought it was mutual. We both agreed that it wasn't working. Over the weekend, I moved out. But when I came in to work the following week, something had changed. I caught people looking my way and then glancing away quickly, whispering in corners and then downright laughing in my face with overtly sexual jokes. I discovered that Penny had sent copies of our intimate conversations in an email to every member of staff, along with a photograph of me in a...compromising...*it was private*," she explained in an almost whisper.

"Wow, that's just...Words fail me."

Catherine nodded. "She was sacked for doing it, but my position was totally untenable, and I had no option but to resign. She contacted me later of course, apologising. She said that she was hurt that I had ended things. I didn't, it was a mutual agreement, but in her mind, I had done her wrong and therefore I should be punished in the worst way possible, by ruining my reputation at work."

Brooke reached for Catherine's hand, the older woman letting her take it and Brooke's thumb rubbing gently over the back of her fingers was reassuring. This was what she wanted.

"I never in a million years expected you to walk through the doors of those interviews." Catherine laughed sardonically. "I should have sat you down and explained all of this, but I was so scared. I know they call me the ice queen and Frosty Knickers; those walls are thin. I hear them all gossiping about other members of staff and I just...I couldn't risk it."

"I'm not going to say this hasn't hurt me," Brooke said, still holding her hand.

"I know...I'm not trying to make excuses. I was a cow when all you were trying to do was be nice and prove your worth. I brushed you off and left you feeling miserable. I did to you what I swore I'd never let anyone else ever do to me, and I am not proud of myself."

"So, you know now that I'd never do that to you, right?" Brooke smiled. The idea of ever causing this woman to hurt in anyway was pretty much unthinkable.

Catherine nodded. "Yes, but there is more. It's not just the work thing."

Brooke was confused. "What else?"

Catherine smiled warmly at her. "Brooke, look at you. You're only 26, the world is out there waiting for you."

Brooke shrugged. "So what? You're ten years older than me, doesn't make a difference to me."

"Oh, you are sweet," she laughed gently. "Brooke, I am 42...I was already having sex before you were even born."

Brooke considered this new information. Catherine didn't look her age, that was for sure. "Then you should have plenty of experience to teach me. The world is out there, and I can see it with you; hell, I've already seen most of it." She stood up, dragged the stool around to Catherine's side of the bar and sat back down on it. "Look, I am not an idiot..."

"I know that..."

"Catherine, can I speak now?"

"Yes, sorry."

"I like you, *a lot.* I find you really attractive. You're sexy, and I think we're pretty compatible, you know, in bed too." She blushed a little, but continued on. "But mostly, I feel this...connection, I feel like..."

Forget it

Catherine reached out for Brooke's face. Taking it in her palms, she leant forward and kissed her softly.

"I feel it, I do...I feel it."

Chapter Forty-Two

Catherine dropped Brooke off at home just after seven that evening. She had wanted to continue talking, but Brooke had things she needed to discuss with Robin as well, and she didn't want to wait.

She found Robin in the living room, sitting cross-legged in Catherine's armchair with a book open in her lap and another hanging off of the arm of the chair. Brooke grinned to herself as she considered the chair belonging to Catherine.

"We need to talk," Brooke said as she entered the room fully. She felt a little peeved at just how easily her sister had manipulated the situation for her own benefit.

Robin jumped. "Jesus, Brooke, you don't have to sneak up like that."

"I wasn't sneaking, unlike you." She sat down on the couch opposite and watched as her sister cringed. "Let's discuss this job of yours."

"Okay, the thing is..." she started, placing her books down on the floor besides her. "Wait, you got your memory back?"

Brooke nodded. "I got my memory back, yes."

"Wow, that's great, we should celebrate," Robin stammered trying to change the subject.

Brooke's stern face told her otherwise. "You used my injury against me so that you could get what you wanted. That's not cool, Robin."

She looked away, biting her lip. "I know, but I just wanted to help. I knew we were struggling, even with you having a new job..."

"Binnie, we talked about this..." She stood again and paced the room.

Robin jumped up. "No, you talked, you decided and I...I'm fifteen, I need to start learning to stand on my own two feet and, Mr Khan's is the best place to take my first steps. It's safe, and it's easy...I get paid my first wage and I can pay some of my way..."

"I get that, but the point is this...this is your big year at school. When you get back after the holidays you've got exams, and you need to be prepared for that."

The youngster picked up a book and held it in the air. "I know, I am studying still. I work one day, and I've already bought my party dress, so that's one less thing you need to worry about. The rest I am putting towards the trip, and Mr Khan said that if I want then I can keep on working after Christmas...just Saturday...I really want to, Brooke," she pleaded. "And I know I shouldn't have used your injury to get what I wanted, but I just thought it made sense...I'd be out of your hair and you had Catherine here...and I thought...I thought, that if you and her had the time again, maybe it would turn out differently."

Brooke had to admit that her kid sister made a compelling argument, even if she had used devious and underhanded tactics. Should she be punished for seeing a solution to something and using it? Brooke would probably have done similar if she had been able to get away with it at that age, and at least now, the dinner for two made sense.

"Okay, here's the deal. You can keep working at Mr Khan's on two conditions. One, you keep your grades up. Any inkling that you are not studying properly, then you stop working there." Robin nodded and tried to hide the grin that was threatening to spread across her face. "And two, you stop interfering in my love life, otherwise I am going to go hang out at the school gates and have a word with Miles."

Robin laughed. "Yeah and get yourself arrested for being a perv." She flopped back down into the chair and picked up her book. When she looked up again through a curtain of hair, she found Brooke still standing there grinning. "Why are you looking so happy? Not that you shouldn't be but... I haven't seen you this happy since...oh my God, you and Catherine? Is it back on?"

"We're talking," Brooke said, letting herself fall backwards onto the couch, her arms outstretched like a kid doing an aeroplane around the room.

Robin fist pumped the air. "Yes, I knew if she just got to spend time with you then..."

Kicking off her boots, Brooke said, "Was this before or after you gave her a hard time?" The raised brow gave Robin half a hint that she wasn't being too serious.

"Well, she needed to know that being a cow to my big sister, wasn't going to cut it with the little sister."

Brooke picked up a magazine and flicked through the pages, lifting her feet up onto the coffee table. She felt content. Life was falling into place at last. Christmas was literally around the corner, and she felt like it wasn't going to be the saddest day on record any longer. She sat up suddenly as realisation hit her.

"What?" Robin asked, noting the movement.

"I just thought, it's Christmas next week." Brooke closed the magazine and placed it tidily on the shelf under the table.

"Yeah, today's the 17th."

"I know but, I've got nothing organised." She jumped up and patted down her pockets. Locating her wallet, she checked the contents. "I need to..." She picked up her phone and scrolled through her contacts until she found the name she wanted. "Amber, are you still at work?" As she listened to Amber talk, she mouthed that she wouldn't be long. Robin waved her off and shook her head, laughing.

Chapter Forty-Three

Finding Amber in the café sipping on a latte, Brooke all but skidded to a halt as she reached the table. "Hey."

"Hello, did you want one?" Amber asked, indicating the coffee.

Brooke shook her head and pulled out a chair to wait. "No, I'm good, thanks. And thanks for doing this."

"Not a problem, do you want company or just whizz round and then I'll join you at the checkout?" Amber asked, sipping her coffee. It was pretty full and still steaming.

"I guess I could get everything while you finish that," Brooke agreed. "I won't be long. Just need to pick up a few things, and the discount you get will be a godsend, seeing as I won't get paid before Christmas."

Amber smiled up at her as she stood, ready to complete her errands. "It's fine, might as well make some use of it. I am at my mum's for Christmas, so other than a few presents, I don't have to buy anything."

"Well, like I say, thanks for this. I won't be too long." She turned then and ran back down the stairs. Getting a trolley from the store's entrance, she waved a quick hello to Stan, before whizzing back inside.

Her first port of call was the music aisle. She grabbed a couple of CDs she knew Robin wanted and picked one of the Christmas albums too; nothing like carols on Christmas morning as they opened their presents. In the clothing section, she found a nice top that would work with most of Robin's skirts or trousers, the obligatory Christmas jumpers, and a dressing gown covered in penguins for Catherine. None of the items was particularly expensive, but that didn't matter.

She found a cute bear for Jasmine and a couple of toys for her siblings. Unsure if they actually celebrated Christmas, she figured that if they didn't, then it would suffice as a small thank you gift anyway. Heading down the wine section, she picked up a couple of bottles, one for Catherine and one for Amber. Then she considered whether it was really the done thing to buy someone's present using their own discount card. Shrugging, she decided needs must and carried on with the shopping, filling the trolley with a few bits that could go into the freezer.

As she rounded the last aisle, she felt her phone buzz in her pocket and she fished it out, smiling when she saw the name: Catherine.

Catherine: How's it going with Robin? Xx

Brooke: I had a good talk with her and now I am at work. Christmas shopping. Xx

Catherine: God, yes, it's almost Christmas. I forgot that. Xx

Brooke: You have seen the store, right? All these fairy lights and elves? Xx

Brooke chuckled as she pushed the trolley towards the tills. She looked up and saw Amber wave her over and pushed the cart in her direction as she read the next text message.

Catherine: Of course, however I have been a little preoccupied with one of my staff members recently. Xx

Brooke: Oh, which one? Xx

Catherine: The hot, sexy one that wears a uniform so well that all I want to do is let her ravish me anytime she visits my office. Xx

Brooke grinned and felt the first flush of arousal fuel her movements as she quickly double-checked her trolley. She didn't want to forget anything.

Brooke: Oh, that one. Yeah, she told me that all she thinks about was the gorgeous HR manager naked in her bed. Xx

The phone beeped once more just as Amber bounded up to her, a blur of purples and pinks wrapped around a smile. Brooke quickly opened the message and found an image along with the latest text.

Catherine: I'm naked in my bed. Xx

Brooke's face flushed at the sight of Catherine's naked torso, the sheet just about covering her lower half, her left-hand snaking beneath it. It was sexy, but more than that, it was trust. Catherine was walking the walk, and that turned Brooke on even more than any naked image could.

"Everything alright?" Amber asked, gazing up at her and waving her discount card in the air to get her attention.

"Yep, all is just...perfect."

With everything packed into carrier bags bearing the name Pollards boldly across either side of them, Amber looked concerned. "How are you getting all of this home?"

"I'll uh...hmm?" Brooke tried to pick them up, but no matter which way she tried, there was no way she could manage it with her wrist still not one hundred percent. She considered calling a taxi, but that wasn't something she could really afford. It would be at least a tenner to get home, and that was money that could be spent on a lot of other things that were more important. It was frustrating to not be able to just carry it all onto the bus.

Amber checked her watch. "Look, I have to get going, get a cab or see if someone upstairs is going your way?" She leant up on tiptoes and kissed Brooke's cheek. "Got a date with Brian." She grinned before skipping off, waving over her shoulder.

"Go, enjoy. I will be fine." She was happy for her friend and watched her hurry away. Pulling her phone from her pocket, she noticed another text from Catherine.

Catherine: Sorry, was that too soon? Xx

She realised that she hadn't replied to the previous text and felt bad for letting Catherine worry.

Brooke: No, I loved it, was just paying at the tills and trying to solve my predicament. Xx

Catherine: What's wrong? Are you okay?

Brooke snapped a photo of her bags and then a different picture of her injured hand.

Brooke: Seven of these and only one of these that works properly. Xx

Catherine: Wait there, I'll be 10 mins xx

She was about to reply and politely refuse. Catherine was in bed. It was only 7p.m., but still, she was clearly settled for the evening. However, Brooke selfishly wanted to see her again. So, she waited outside in the cold, grinning when she saw the black SUV pull into the kerb outside almost fifteen minutes later.

Catherine jumped out and had the boot open in seconds, coming around the car to help load the bags. "You should have said. I'd have taken you shopping," she said, reaching out to take another bag from Brooke's hand. "I really wouldn't have minded."

"I know, but I hadn't even thought about it, and..." She smiled shyly. "I needed presents."

"Yes, and I could have helped with that."

Brooke blushed and looked away. "But then it wouldn't be a surprise," she mumbled.

"What do you mean?" When Brooke said nothing but raised a brow, she got it. "Oh, you bought something for me?"

Dark hair nodded as the last bag went into the boot. "It's nothing exciting, I just thought..."

Catherine climbed into the car and waited as Brooke followed. When she was settled in her seat, Catherine leant across and used her finger to turn Brooke's chin towards her. "I will love it." she whispered, leaning forward to kiss her.

The blare of a horn from behind broke the spell as an impatient taxi wanted to get out from behind Catherine's car. She smiled against Brooke's lips.

"I guess that means we should get moving."

Brooke grinned. "Make him wait." And she leant into kiss her once more. Both of them broke into laughter as the Hornblower blared again. Catherine waved back at him and pulled her car away from the kerb.

"Some people are so impatient." Brooke laughed, her good hand resting easily on Catherine's thigh as she drove.

Chapter Forty-Four

Catherine took the lead and carried the heaviest bags up the stairs, holding doors for Brooke and receiving a kiss at each pass. She felt lighter in herself since their heart-to-heart. She had decided that Ronnie was right: at some point, she was going to have to just trust that the person in her life would be as honourable as she hoped they would be. So far, Brooke had done nothing to prove otherwise, and as Catherine stood in the hallway outside of Brooke's flat, waiting as Brooke trudged along laden down with bags that she wouldn't let Catherine anywhere near, she couldn't help but feel a rush of desire and lust pulse its way through her lower regions.

When Brooke caught up, she dropped the bags gently to the floor and leant forward, capturing smiling lips and holding them hostage until her tongue made a rescue attempt. "I like it when you're all casual like this," Brooke said. Catherine in blue jeans and leather jacket was a look the blonde carried off too well.

"I'll wear it again then." She grinned and leaned against Brooke's back as she pulled her keys from her pocket.

"Uh huh, mind you, I think I prefer you in just your underwear."

Catherine leant in further and smouldered against her ear. "I'm not wearing any."

She laughed out loud when she heard the gasp of "Fuck" skitter from Brooke's mouth while she fumbled with the key in the lock. She pushed the door open and held it for Catherine to pass through. The blonde shrugged off her jacket while Brooke brought her bags inside. Kicking off her high tops, her bare feet pitter-pattered along the hallway and into the lounge.

Robin looked up from her seat, still reading, but a different book this time. A notepad was open beside her with several notes scribbled in biro. "Hey Catherine."

"Hello, Robin." She tilted her head to see what it was that she was reading. *Pride and Prejudice*. "Good book?"

Robin twisted the book around to look at the cover. "It's okay..." she sighed. "I wanted to read *The War of the Worlds*, but we all voted and this won." Her nose scrunched up as she shrugged.

They both looked around at the sound of Brooke swearing and crashing bags against the walls. "Do you want help?" Catherine called out.

"No, all good. Just have to put these ones in my room, and then the other two need to be packed way in the freezer and I am all yours," Brooke called back. Gently toeing the door to her room open, she propped the bags up against her chest of drawers. As she straightened, she felt the warm arms snake around her waist, soft breasts pressing up against her back.

"Do you think Robin would mind if we stayed in here all evening, naked and writhing in your bed?"

Brooke turned in Catherine's arms, studying her face, the way her eyes sparkled when she smiled like that. "You're so sexy. Stay the night?"

The groan that left Catherine's lips was downright sinful. "I really want to."

"But?"

Catherine smiled. "I don't have a change of clothes."

"So? There is no dress code for office staff, otherwise Amber would not be allowed to enter the building." Brooke grinned and leant in to place a soft kiss against the corner of Catherine's mouth.

"I can't go to work in jeans," Catherine gasped.

"Oh the shame of it!" mocked Brooke. "You look hot, you look relaxed, and I'm gonna be honest, it's clear that you've been trying to cultivate a...nicer you at the office."

Catherine playfully slapped her arm. "I'm always...okay fine, yes I want to be nicer, but that doesn't mean I need to look like a slob."

Brooke looked down at her own jeans and shirt ensemble. "A slob?"

Realising the mistake, Catherine chuckled. "Of course, you look amazing in jeans and being the rugged, protective and strong security guard that you are, it's the perfect getup."

Brooke took Catherine's hand and led her over to the mirror. It hung perfectly on the wall to give a full-length image of them both: Brooke standing behind, her arms wrapping around Catherine's waist as her chin tucked into the curve of her neck. "Just look at you."

Catherine tried to turn away, but Brooke put a fingertip to her chin and directed her attention back to the mirror. "You're gorgeous. There is nothing about you that needs to be hidden behind fancy clothes and an ice queen exterior."

Catherine studied herself, trying to see what Brooke saw. Closing her eyes, she imagined herself walking into work the next day wearing this outfit, passing Stan and waving hello. Brooke's lips were warm as they kissed the patch of skin between her shoulder blades. Her left hand, still bandaged, slid beneath Catherine's shirt, flattening out against the softness of her stomach.

She inhaled, exhaled, and then opened her eyes and watched as Brooke's mouth began to move against the curve of her shoulder, up the taut tendon in her neck.

"Keep doing that." She whimpered and relaxed against her as their eyes met in the mirror and held until Brooke moved on with her kisses and Catherine's gaze followed her lips. She hadn't even noticed the right hand joining the left until both were cupping her braless breasts. She dropped her gaze lower and watched as her own hands, working with a mind of their own, undid the button on her jeans, loosening the zipper before reaching for Brooke's good hand, urging it down and away from the nipple it was currently teasing.

"Why don't you come back to my place?" Catherine asked, pushing her jeans down lower to give her lover more room. She gasped each time Brooke teased a finger pad against her clit.

"Can't...can't leave...Robin," Brooke said, moaning against her ear as her finger dipped lower, into the wetness of her. "You feel so good."

Catherine studied the image in front of her: her jeans half way down her thighs, her lover's hand between her slightly parted legs, moving against her as she gently thrust her hips back and forth. Brooke's other hand moved across her chest beneath her shirt, caressing one breast and then the other. She could see her nipples straining against the material, the contrast of dark next to blonde, tan skin against pale. Just watching them together was turning her on. She bit down the urge to cry out as Brooke increased the pressure and speed of her movements.

"Make me—" Her words caught in her throat as Brooke found the one spot that would drive her over the edge. She grabbed at Brooke's thighs, fingers gripping her jeans and grounding her as her breaths came hard and fast, muscles tensing and relaxing at will. "Going to...oh God, right there."

Chapter Forty-Five

Brooke stretched out and felt the empty but warm spot next to her. She sat up, blinked against the darkness, and noticed the shadow of movement as Catherine dressed with just the light from her phone.

"Go back to sleep, you've got another hour," she whispered as she walked topless towards the bed. One knee knelt on the mattress as she leaned in and found sleepy lips.

"Where are you going?" croaked Brooke. She rubbed at her face and the sleep in her eyes.

"Home, I need to get a shower and a change of clothes."

Brooke pulled her down on top of her as she fell back against the pillows. "Want you to stay, let's phone in sick."

Catherine laughed. "You are a bad influence." She kissed her quickly before climbing off of the bed. "Go back to sleep and I will see you in the office at 9."

Brooke was already asleep by the time Catherine snuck out of the bedroom.

~FI~

Getting into the office at just after 8.30, Brooke found Amber and Kim with concerned looks on their faces.

"What's the matter with you two?"

Amber shrugged. "Nothing, it's just Catherine isn't here."

Brooke frowned and checked her watch. "Maybe she's just running late. There was plenty of traffic when I came in on the bus."

"She's never late though," Kim said.

"Well, there was that time when she stormed in here and demanded we got Brooke in the off..." Amber tailed off, realising it wasn't a good point.

Brooke now remembered the day all too well. She didn't want a repeat of that ever again. But that couldn't be the reason now. Catherine had left this morning in a good mood. "I'm just going to go and grab a coffee," she said, pulling her phone from her pocket as she left.

It rang for longer than Brooke was comfortable with, but just as she was about to hang up and redial, Catherine answered.

"Hello?"

"Catherine, where are you?"

There was a pause before she answered. "In my car. In the car park." Brooke sped up, her feet taking the stairs two at a time.

"Are you alright?"

"Uh, yes...yes I'm okay, I just..." She took a deep breath and then another. "I'm nervous."

"Nervous? What about?" Reaching the bottom of the stairwell, she pushed open the emergency exit door that led out to the carpark and looked around for Catherine's car, easily spotting the monster; it towered above most of the others in the area. She moved swiftly towards it.

"I took your advice and now..." She jumped as Brooke rapped her knuckles against the window and put the phone back into her pocket.

Brooke stared in at her through the window and grinned. She was wearing jeans and a cashmere jumper. When the door unlocked, Brooke pulled it open and held out her hand. "Come on. You can do this."

"I can." She took Brooke's hand with one hand and grabbed her bag with the other. "I can do this."

Brooke chuckled. "Yes you can, because you are Catherine Blake, sexy HR manager and the hottest member of staff on the payroll."

Catherine rolled her eyes. "Seriously, has that worked for you before?"

"Oh yeah, all the time." Brooke laughed and guided her by the elbow towards the door. "Now, do you want me to walk in with you, or give you a few minutes to get up there before I return?"

Catherine turned towards her and cupped her cheek. "You really don't mind keeping us a secret for now?"

"I'm not interested in what any member of staff thinks about my love life. I'm only interested in you. And if you need privacy, then so be it."

Catherine kissed her, the kind of kiss that told you that you were loved. The type of kiss that in a private bedroom would lead to one or both of you being naked.

"Thank you for making me want to be the person I know I can be again."

Forget it

"You're doing that all by yourself."

~FI~

Walking into the office was the most daunting thing Catherine had done in a long time. She'd slowed her pace as she walked the corridor and neared the door. Taking a deep breath, she tried to remember back, before Penny, when she was happier. Brooke was giving her a 5-minute head start, and she was determined to be in her office and over herself before Brooke arrived.

"Fake it," she mumbled to herself. If she could just fake it now, then it would come more easily over time. She turned the corner, fully expecting the gasps of surprise from Amber and Kim. "Morning," she said brightly.

Amber was at the kettle waiting for it to boil. "Morning, Catherine. Tea?"

"I'd love one, thank you."

"Good morning," Kim said, looking up from her phone.

"I'll be in my office if anyone needs me," Catherine added, startled that neither woman had commented on her lack of suitable office attire.

"Okie dokie. I'll bring your tea in when it's made." Amber smiled. "Oh, and I changed the time of your meeting this morning. Mr Sims called, and he is stuck in traffic."

"Brilliant, thank you." She was about to enter her office when she stopped. "I wondered if either of you would like to join me for lunch today?"

She held her breath and waited as both women looked at each other. During the awkward silence, Brooke strolled in and took in the scene.

"That would be lovely actually, thanks Catherine," Kim finally said, smiling at her.

"Yes, that would definitely be preferable to spending an entire hour with Brooke." Amber winked at her friend.

"Hey, that's rude. What are we all doing? Am I invited?" Brooke asked.

Catherine smiled at the scene; it was pretty easy once she let herself relax. "Of course, you're paying." She entered her office, laughing at the stunned look on Brooke's face.

Chapter Forty-Six

"Robin, if you don't hurry up, the poor kid is going to be standing outside wondering if he should have bothered," Brooke said through the bathroom door. "Or shall I invite him in? I'm sure we could find loads to talk about."

The door flung open to reveal Robin in a beautiful red dress and low heels with her hair piled up on her head. "Don't you dare."

Brooke sniggered before sobering. "You look amazing."

"Ya think so?" the teen asked, twirling around in the hallway. "Let me see what Catherine thinks."

"Oh, my opinion not good enough?" Brooke laughed, following her into the lounge, where Catherine was giving her the once-over. "Well, does she pass?"

Catherine smiled and held Robin by the shoulders. "You look beautiful, and if Miles doesn't appreciate it, then he doesn't deserve you."

"Thanks," Robin said, looking between the two of them. "I guess I'd better go then."

"Have fun, don't be late, and if he does anything that you're not comfortable with, then you call me and we will come and get you," Brooke was saying as she followed her sister down the hallway.

Robin pulled on her coat and grabbed her keys. "He won't, but I will call if anything happens." She kissed Brooke on the cheek. "Thanks, B."

Brooke held the door open and listened as Robin descended the stairs. When she reached the bottom and the door opened, she smiled to herself as she heard the deep voice of Miles tell her she looked gorgeous.

"Brooke, she will be fine," Catherine said. She stood at the other end of the hall, watching her girlfriend being all protective.

"I know, it's just...it was only last week that she was four." Brooke smiled wryly. "Now she's got her first boyfriend, and you know what is going to come next? Her first broken heart, and I'm not sure I know how to deal with that."

Catherine walked towards her. "You will deal with it, because you're her sister and she looks up to you." As she reached her, she let her arms snake up around Brooke's neck and kissed the corner of her mouth. "Come on, we have a film to watch."

~Fl~

The film was over two hours ago, and Brooke was fidgety. She had been up and down for the last 30 minutes, checking out of the window, making tea, checking the window again.

"Brooke, she isn't even due home for another 40 minutes!" Catherine chuckled.

"Well, they just walked up the path," she said, peeping out around the curtain. "What are they doing?" She observed them as they stood together in the lamplight, smiling at each other. "Oh God," Brooke realised. "This is that awkward moment when they might kiss, isn't it?"

Catherine laughed. "Brooke, are you seriously going to stand there and watch them have their moment?"

Brooke glanced back at her lover. "Yes...No." It was like car crash TV; she couldn't look away and yet, she didn't want to see it.

"Come here and let me take your mind off of it," Catherine said, holding out a hand for Brooke to take, which she finally did. "Now, come sit here." Catherine tugged her right hand until she gave in and sat down on the couch. In a swift move that Brooke wasn't expecting, Catherine settled herself in her lap, straddling her thighs.

"I see, so your plan is to trap me in the sofa?"

"Yes, it's a good plan." She smiled, leaning in to take Brooke's lips in a gentle kiss. "As plans go, I am quite proud of this one." The one thing Catherine had learnt early on with Brooke was just how much she enjoyed kissing her. Sliding her tongue into her mouth and grinding down against her, she kept her mind from wandering until the sound of the key in the lock put pay to Brooke's relaxed state. Catherine slid elegantly off of her lap and into the seat next to her as though she had never been sitting anywhere else. Keeping hold of her shirt, she snuggled into her flank. "Just sit here and wait for her to come in. Pretend you're not bothered."

"But I am bothered." Brooke checked her watch. "They were down there for nearly 15 minutes." The sound of Robin kicking off her shoes reverberated down the hallway. "She's just a kid."

"Doing exactly what we were doing," Catherine reminded.

"Yeah, well that's the point isn't it? I know where I was planning to go next."

Catherine laughed out loud. "So did she: home!"

Before Brooke could comment again, Robin came into the room, blowing her cheeks out. She looked flushed and dreamy.

"Nice time?" Catherine asked, squeezing Brooke around the middle.

Robin nodded. "The best. It was so much fun. Jas and Simeon were making everyone laugh. And then some idiot tried to spike the punch with vodka, but Miles caught them and saved the day." She flopped down into the armchair and sighed.

Catherine gently pinched Brooke's side and leaned in to kiss her cheek. "See, he's a good kid," she whispered, before adding, "Take me to bed."

"Right," Brooke said, suddenly standing and holding her hand out for Catherine. "We will see you in the morning then?"

Robin nodded. Standing herself, she reached out and wrapped her arms around Brooke. "Thanks,"

"What for?"

"For being my sister and not turning into some overbearing parent figure that doesn't want me to grow up."

Catherine sniggered. "I'm off to bed. Night, Robin."

"Night, Catherine." Robin smiled. "Oh, are you coming to Christmas dinner?"

Catherine raised her eyebrows in Brooke's direction. "I don't know, am I?"

"I'd like it if you did, I just didn't want to assume you would." Brooke grinned.

"Well, I am pretty sure that I told you before, you can assume whatever you like," Catherine purred.

"Oh, get a room." Robin laughed and rushed past them to the sanctuary of her own room.

"Actually, I think you said that I could take liberties with you," Brooke corrected.

Thinking back to that night weeks ago at Art, Catherine said, "I think you might be right. Your memory is definitely back then."

Brooke grinned, nodding. She took Catherine's hand and led her through to her own room. "And, my wrist is working just fine too." She waggled it to prove the point.

"Oh, well in that case..." Catherine giggled as Brooke toed the door open and made a grab for her. "You're overdressed."

Chapter Forty-Seven

As Christmas Eves went, this was turning out to be one of the best Brooke had ever witnessed, not counting the year she finally got a Mr Frosty in her sack from Santa.

Robin was out on a double date with Miles, Jas, and Simeon. That meant that Catherine had come over, ready to spend the entire three days of Christmas together. Brooke had created a new Chambers tradition: fish and chip take away dinner, with cans of pre-mixed cocktails and a tub of ice cream.

They had eaten dinner on their laps out of the paper it was wrapped in, while James Bond entertained on the TV, but the ice cream was currently being smeared across Catherine's torso. Brooke licked the melting salted caramel as it ran in slow icy drips to pool at Catherine's belly button.

"This is definitely the best way..." Her tongue swiped and dipped. "...to eat ice cream." She grinned, licking her lips before dipping down to clean up the rest.

"Uh huh. I can say it's certainly an experience." Catherine writhed gently under the teasing strokes of Brooke's tongue. "Feel free to extend the buffet table."

Brooke laughed. Picking up the pot of now soft and very melted cold liquid, she dripped it strategically between folds and chuckled as Catherine gasped, first at the coolness and then at the attention Brooke's mouth was giving her.

~Fl~

Forget it

It was cosy and warm as Brooke burrowed deeper under the duvet, pressing up against the warmth of Catherine as she lay equally snug. Brooke lay there quietly and listened for any sound in the house. There was noise coming from somewhere, a low hum. As she listened more, the giveaway click of the kettle reaching its boiling point could just be heard. She needed to remember just how thin these walls were. Catherine rolled over and mumbled in her sleep, and Brooke couldn't keep the grin from her face.

Reaching over, Brooke found her phone and checked the time. Just after 9 a.m. Placing a kiss against Catherine's forehead, she slid gently out of bed and re-wrapped Catherine under the covers. It had been a late one for them, she thought as she grinned at the memories.

Stretching out, she yawned and reached for her old work out trackies, pulling them on quickly to escape the cold. She found a clean hoodie and yanked it over her head. grateful to no longer be wincing at every movement. At this rate, she would be back to work in the new year, and Catherine had hinted at outing them both to colleagues. Not that Brooke was that bothered. She had confided in Amber of course, and she just wanted to double date, now that she was seeing Brian.

Brooke shuffled into the kitchen and found Robin in her usual spot, in front of the oven. She had a jug of eggs whisked, and a plate of raw sausages and bacon ready to fry.

"Catherine's a vegetarian," Brooke said to Robin's back. The teen stiffened and turned quickly.

"What? Why has nobody told me this? Oh my God."

Brooke laughed. "Just kidding."

Robin tossed the tea towel at her and scowled. "You're such a shit."

"I know, but your face..." Brooke continued to laugh.

"Did you want breakfast?" Robin asked, in all seriousness. She was the one cooking after all, and she could easily stop.

"Uh, okay...I'll just...I'll wake Catherine up then."

"Yeah, you do that, and then you can set the table... and don't forget Dad."

Brooke stopped smiling. "I won't. Head of the table, right?"

Robin only nodded, before turning back to finish her task. Scrambled eggs, bacon and sausages, with mushrooms and toast. The Chambers Christmas Breakfast!

~FI~

Brooke slipped back into her room and crept over to the bed. Sliding back in under the covers, she pressed up against Catherine's sleeping form once more.

"Morning, Baby," she whispered, placing gentle kisses along her bare shoulder. "It's Christmas morning and time to get up." More kisses, this time the pressure a little firmer. Catherine groaned, moving her head to make room for those kisses to spread to her neck. "Catherine, Sweetheart?"

"Mm nice, don't stop," she mumbled, and Brooke giggled. Catherine rolled backwards, lying supine under Brooke's now-hovering body. Her eyes flickered open in the dim light. "Come back to bed."

Brooke smiled and shook her head. "Can't, Robin is cooking breakfast and you're invited to attend."

Catherine rubbed her face and yawned. A piece of hair lay across her forehead and Brooke moved it aside, placing a kiss where it had been, then another on her nose, before finally kissing her mouth. "Hmm, maybe we both need to brush our teeth." She laughed and earned a playful slap.

"Fine, I'm getting up." Catherine smiled but didn't make any effort to move. "Merry Christmas, Darling."

"Merry Christmas, wanna share a shower? I think we've got approximately five more minutes, but I reckon we can stretch it to seven."

~FI~

Breakfast was beyond amazing, and both Catherine and Brooke were quick to heap praise on Robin. The youngster had been a little subdued, which Brooke assumed was to do with their dad not being there. She wasn't sure what more she could do about that other than to just let Robin have her quiet time and try to nudge her out of her funk throughout the day.

"So, presents now or later?" Brooke asked as Catherine cleared the dishes and stacked them by the sink for Brooke to wash.

"I don't mind," she said over her shoulder. "What do you want to do, Robin?"

The teenager shrugged. "I guess we could do them now."

Brooke jumped up. "Great," she said excitedly, and Catherine couldn't help but enjoy the exuberance. "I'll get them out from under the tree, meet you in the lounge when you're ready."

With Brooke gone, Catherine took the opportunity to speak with Robin. "Everything okay?" she asked, wiping her hands on the towel.

Robin looked up, surprised by the question. "Yeah, just...I was thinking about my mum."

"Oh." Catherine wasn't sure what to say. She didn't know much about the woman. Brooke rarely mentioned her, and the only things she did know had been from asking questions. She sat back down in her chair and poured another cup of tea from the pot.

"It's just, normally I don't think about her, well, rarely...she made her choices and they don't involve us," she explained as Catherine listened. "It's been really nice having you here, and we've been like a proper family. I know that you're Brooke's girlfriend, but I know that you're older than her too, and..."

"I'm not your mum, Robin, and I'd never want to take her place, but if you ever feel like you need someone else to talk to, someone other than Brooke, I am here." She reached out and took Robin's hand. She didn't know how things would work out with Brooke; she hoped for the best, but she was pragmatic enough to know that things could change.

"Thanks, I just miss them both. My Dad's dead and my Mum might as well be." She shrugged again.

"I am sure that on days like today, she thinks of you both too."

Robin scoffed, "Doubt it, she's a very selfish woman, Catherine."

The older woman nodded. "Well, in that case, I think what we have to do is make sure that we have as much fun as we can. Starting with opening presents, come on." She stood and grabbed Robin's hand. "I know for a fact there are quite a few for you!"

~FI~

Wrapping paper covered the carpet as presents were unwrapped, ooed over, and then placed neatly in a pile while the next was passed over for opening. Brooke grinned as Robin ripped open the gifts and squealed at the new CDs and tops. She was even more excited when she opened Catherine's gift, a new pair of trainers that cost more than Robin had earned in a month.

"Oh, wow. Thank you so much," she gushed as she threw her arms around Catherine. "Jas is going to be so jealous."

"Well, there is a little something for her too, if you would give it to her when you see her."

"Thank you!"

They both turned to watch as Brooke lifted her present from Catherine.

She made a big deal of lifting it, listening to it, and shaking it gently as she tried to work out what it was. It was a big box, but it was really light and silent.

"Oh, come on, B." Robin laughed. "Just open it, how can you stand it?"

Finally, she ripped the paper off and opened the box. Pulling out tissue paper, she raised a brow. "Is this box empty?"

Catherine laughed. "No."

Eventually, she came to the bottom and found an envelope stuck down. She gently pulled it free and inspected it. It was sealed with a lipstick mark. "Yours, I hope." She chuckled as Catherine nodded. She slid a finger under the lip and eased the glue free to reveal a piece of paper, folded into three. "'This certificate gives the bearer, Brooke Chambers, the option of two weeks in the sun with Catherine Blake somewhere hot and exotic.' What? really?"

"Yes, I spoke with Robin and she already checked with Mrs Khan. Once we pick dates, she can stay with them, and we can spend a romantic two weeks lying in the..." She was cut off as Brooke leant across the discarded box to plant a kiss on her lips.

Robin stood up, laughing at them. "Get a room."

Epilogue

The sun beat down on already tanned skin, shining beneath a sheen of oil and sweat. Catherine rolled over onto her front and leant up on her elbows to continue reading her book. Her attention was caught by movement in front of her. She placed the book down and looked up to see Brooke emerging from the pool. Her hair was longer now and was swept back off her face, dripping droplets of water onto her shoulder. She glistened in the sunshine and grinned as she stalked back to the sunbeds, naked.

"Hey," Catherine said, shielding her eyes from the sun. She would never tire of looking at this woman, clothed or naked. "Good swim?"

"Yeah," Brooke replied. Flopping down on the plastic bed, she used the towel to dab at her skin. "It's so warm in there."

"Hmm, well it's 34 degrees today, so I should think it will be quite warm." It had been the perfect idea to rent a private villa rather than stay at a hotel. They had the pool to themselves and had made quite the most of it since their arrival.

"I think you should join me next time."

"Maybe I will... but first, I need a drink. Would you like one?"

Brooke leant back on her palms and watched, mesmerised as Catherine's naked backside passed her by. "Yes, please."

Catherine reached for a robe and pulled it on. The thin material clung to her skin, and Brooke considered just how sexy the image was. She gave in and got up, following her lover back into the villa.

Catherine gasped as Brooke reached around from behind and hugged her close. "I think that the only thing I need to drink right now, is you."

"Oh." Catherine giggled. Turning in her arms, she found Brooke's lips in an instant. Making no effort to stop her from kissing her, she melted into it. She made no effort to stop Brooke from lifting her onto the counter top, inserting herself between her thighs. She wrapped them around Brooke's waist, trapping her there as they continued to kiss and enjoy one another. "I was thinking," Catherine said between kisses. "We've been together for eight months."

"Uh huh," Brooke said. Kissing a trail down Catherine's neck, she let her tongue slide along the dips of her collarbone.

"And, I thought maybe..." She groaned as Brooke's warm mouth wrapped around her stiffened nipple and sucked gently, her tongue licking it over and over until she could barely concentrate. "Move in with me," She finally got out.

Brooke stopped in her tracks and stood back up. "Seriously? What about Robin?"

"I have three bedrooms. She can choose which of the spare ones she would like." Her palms cupped Brooke's face. "I think we could...it would work, wouldn't it? Me and you, we work. This, it's...it's what I want...permanently."

"I want that too. But I need to see that Robin is okay with it."

Catherine nodded, her eyes glancing shyly to the floor.

Brooke titled Catherine's chin upwards and made eye contact. "I love you and I want to spend my life with you," she admitted. "And Robin loves you too, so I don't foresee there being a negative answer to the question, but she insists that I stop thinking of her as four years old." She smiled, and Catherine chuckled at the joke. "I want to wake up with you everyday."

Catherine smiled and kissed her once more. "I love you." She fingered the small penguin pendant Brooke had gotten her for Christmas. "Penguins mate for life, right?".

ABOUT THE AUTHOR

Claire Highton-Stevenson is a contemporary romance writer in the Lesfic genre.

She is from the UK but often her books are set in the States. She loves to travel and often places that she visits appear in the pages of a story.

When Claire isn't writing, she can be found lurking on social media, watching football (It's not Soccer) and enjoying time with her friends and family.

Claire is married and has 4 fur babies to look after.

If you have enjoyed this book then please consider leaving a review.
Amazon: getbook.at/ForgetITCHS

You can also subscribe to Claire's newsletter
www.itsclastofficial.co.uk

And you can follow Claire on social media.
Twitter : @clastevofficial
Facebook: Claire Highton-Stevenson
Instagram: itsclastevofficial

Now read on for a sample of Claire's other books, Escape and Freedom, and The Doll Maker.

Escape and Freedom

One

Wembley Arena was filled to the rafters with teenagers and parents alike. Every seat in the house had sold out within minutes of being on sale. The sound system rocked the very foundations as the band began to play, kids screaming in expectation. The bassists and guitarists found the beat of the drum and on she walked through the dry ice and bright lights. The crowd erupted again as the lead singer of Solar Flare threw out a "Hello Wembley!"

Song after song after song played out. Nobody sat in their seat; they danced in the aisles instead. It was loud and fun, the band enjoying the show just as much as the audience were.

Lucy Owen was stunning. Her long bleached-blonde hair swept up and to the side, her green eyes shone with anticipation and excitement as she stood there in the centre of the stage and gave her all, the centre of everybody's attention. This was what it was all about: all the hard work and constant rehearsals, nights in the bus, back and forth from one town to the next. It was all for this: this atmosphere, this moment where it all came together, and she was the star.

The music pumped like a heartbeat that thrummed through your very core. Voices rang out, singing and screaming as the concert goers were whipped up into a frenzy of excitement. When a number of them were allowed to come on stage and sing with the band, it was euphoric.

It was the last night of an exhausting European leg of their world tour, and Solar Flare was looking forward to a few weeks off as they headed to America for a series of concerts that would catapult them to superstardom. Their first two albums had gone straight to number one and they were already a hit on both sides of the pond, but this would be the first time they had toured there, and nobody could wait!

When the curtain finally came down and they walked off stage to find their dressing rooms, Lucy Owen was pumped. The guys were all talking about hitting the bar once they got back to their hotel, but she had other ideas on how to spend tonight.

The plan was simple: they were to grab quick showers and get changed, then jump on-board their tour bus and be driven to Heathrow, where they would be staying in a 5-star hotel for the night. In the morning all of them would be flying straight out to the States. Once there, they would get 3 weeks to themselves before the tour prep started and a 63-date tour began. It was going to be the most hectic and tiring time of their lives, but it would also be the most exhilarating and adrenaline-filled time too.

All of them had dreams, and every single one of them took them to America.

British acts didn't do well in the US that often, but when they did, it was the bigtime, and that was what Solar Flare was aiming for. They had worked hard. For 3 long years they had either been on the road touring or in the studio recording, and it had been torturous at times for all of them. They lived together, ate together, slept together too at times when all they could do was grab a few hours on sofas and chairs. They were a family; they had their share of arguments and disagreements, but on the whole, they were having a blast.

Lucy's girlfriend Nicky was going with them and was already waiting for her in the dressing room. Her own mother had described her as tall and gangly, but to Lucy, she was gorgeous. Not just ordinary gorgeous, but the kind that comes along once in a lifetime kind of gorgeous. Her mocha-coloured skin glowed with a light sheen of sweat she had worked up dancing backstage. She was a long drink of something hot, rich, and vibrant that set Lucy's mind racing with all kinds of possibilities. They were a striking couple, their skin tones complementing each other perfectly. They were a yin and yang, dark and light, but they shared the colour green in their eyes, almost exactly the same hue. They had to keep their relationship under the radar as far as the media was concerned, but everyone they knew was aware that they were in love, hopelessly.

"Baby, you were fucking brilliant!" Nicky said, her accent perfectly British unlike Lucy's more common approach to the vernacular. She threw her arms around her neck and kissed her hard. "God, it makes me so horny watching you on stage."

"Yeah? I hadn't noticed." Lucy laughed. "However, we don't have time," she replied, smirking at the pout she knew she had just caused. "Oh, come on now." she said, lifting Nicky's chin and staring into luminous green eyes, "You know that once we get to the hotel I am going to make it up to you?"

"You had better, darling," Nicky said, smiling. "I am horny as fuck right now," she whispered against the shell of her lover's ear, sending delightful shivers of anticipation down Lucy's spine in an instant.

It always amused Lucy whenever Nicky used such crass language. Her father had been born and raised in Jamaica, but had joined the British army at an early age, and that was where he had met her mother, while stationed in the UK. Looking at her and the way she dressed, the people she chose to hang out with, you would never guess that Nicky had been raised and educated in some of the best schools money could buy, until she spoke. When she did speak, it was eloquent, and every word was enunciated correctly, meaning that when she did choose to swear, it was fundamentally more enticing than anything anyone else could have said to Lucy.

A loud banging on the door followed by a deep voice bellowing, "Five minutes and we're leaving!" ended the moment.

"Let's just leg it and go to the airport by ourselves later," Nicky suggested with a wink.

"You know we can't do that, anyway it will be fun on the bus with the guys, a last hurrah," Lucy argued. "They've got cham-pag-ne," she sing-sang as she teased, knowing just how much Nicky loved to drink the bubbly stuff.

"I guess so. Why do I always let you get your own way, huh?" Her palm caressed Lucy's cheek.

"Because I love you?" she smirked, kissing her quickly.

"I love you more," Nicky countered, kissing the corner of her mouth once again.

"I doubt it."

"Oh, it's true, who else would put up with all the teenage boys that want to have their way with you?"

"Well, they don't get to, do they?" Lucy challenged, raising an eyebrow and the sexual tension as they kissed once more. Lucy tugged Nicky's body into her own by her belt loops. Someone banged on the door again, and this time it opened when Scott popped in and jerked his head towards the hallway. "Come on, we're off," he said. "USA here we come!" he continued to shout as he moved on to the next door down the hall.

They smiled at one another before both grabbed their bags and then, holding hands, they ran for the bus, laughing as they stumbled along the corridor.

There was a small group of about 50 fans outside, and they had to run the gauntlet to get through it. People always wanted to touch her, grab at her, talk to her, and on the whole, she accepted that as part of the job, but right now she just wanted to get to the hotel and spend a few hours naked with the woman she adored before hours of travelling and jet lag took its toll.

~E&F~

Greeted by whoops and high fives from the guys as they finally clambered aboard, they were all still bouncing on the adrenaline a show provoked. Scott played bass along with Jenna; Sarah and Ben played the drums; Chris, Rob and Mike played various guitars; and Sasha played keyboards. Lucy played the piano too, but she was the lead singer with the other guys all having their moments on the mic. Jenna, Sarah, and Chris did most of the backing and between them, they had a fantastic sound. A sound that was going to transcend the Atlantic and bring them worldwide success.

Someone opened a bottle of champagne, the loud pop of the cork causing more whoops and cheers. Plastic glasses filled quickly as they all toasted each other, all except Sasha. She was strapped in and taking a nap like she always did after a show. They toasted the end of this part of the tour and for further success in the future, swallowing down the liquid in one. They were cruising, through life and along the motorway.

They were young, famous and rich, with the world at their feet one minute and in the next, it all came crashing down, literally.

Two

There had been no time to even think about what was happening. It was a small bump, barely noticeable, and then the bus careered out of its lane, skidding back and forth, tossing them around a little in their seats and down the aisle as the driver tried desperately to get it back under control, but it was too late. The road was wet from an earlier shower and the wheels had locked up, forcing the cumbersome vehicle into a skid. The back of the bus where all the weight was held swung violently into the central reservation and pushed the front of it out of control even more. The driver slammed on the brakes in a last-ditch attempt to gain control, but all that did was cause them to lock up further, and the bus rolled over onto its side. What had once been windows and a wall was now the floor as the bus careered along the ground at speed. Sparks flew as the metal came into contact with the tarmac. Its occupants were thrown around like rag dolls in a dog's mouth. Glass shattered as windows hit and then imploded on impact. Boxes and bags that had been held in overhead compartments were now tossed around hitting anyone in their way. The cacophony of metal scraping was like a painful screech. Finally, the roof buckled as the motorway bridge pillar halted its forward momentum with an almighty crash, stopping it from sliding any further, crushing anything in its path.

The impact was earth-shattering. There was silence for just a moment and then the screams, the terrifying god-awful screaming of people hurt and frightened. Debris was strewn across the road leading a trail of destruction to the mangled and crushed vehicle.

A mere 45 seconds had felt like a lifetime, the power of the event monumental in its destruction. Lives that were full of promise and expectation just evaporated in a heartbeat that stopped dancing to its own rhythm, to any rhythm. Nothing would be the same again, for any of them or anyone connected to them.

~E&F~

Blue and red lights flashed around her. It was almost hypnotic, the way the colours danced around and over one another like a ballet of light that lit up everything for a second, before plunging into darkness once more. Over and over the colours swept across her. One minute there had been silence and then the roar of screams and machinery had deafened her. Her hands covered her ears and she felt warm tears slide down her face. She heard herself call for Nicky, but she couldn't hear a reply through all of the noise.

And there was pain, a lot of pain, and yet, she couldn't pinpoint where from; it was everywhere all at once. She tried to concentrate on each part of herself, to locate the epicentre of the agony. Her leg definitely hurt, her head hurt too, and when she tried to move she found she was pinned down. At some point, she tried to move again, and the pain that shot through her was so intense that it caused her to pass out.

The next time that she came around, she realised that she was still on the bus and a paramedic was attending to her. She had no concept of time; it could have been a minute, it might have been a day, and she didn't know or care. She had no clue as to what had happened other than the obvious. Something was sticking in her arm, she knew that much; a drip maybe? And she was asking where Nicky was, but he just kept talking to her about her injuries. It was frustrating, and she was getting more worked up and annoyed. The paramedic was explaining that they had to move her.

It all went black.

Three

Everything was bright, so very bright. When she tried to open her eyes, that was the only thought she had: too bright. Her head pounded when she rolled it to the left. A window. Blinds open and the sunshine was streaming through so clearly, she could see dust particles hanging in the haze of it. It was confusing. She didn't remember making it to the hotel or going to bed, and she was definitely in a bed. Taking a deep breath, she rolled her head the other way and tried to work out what the machines were for. She tried lifting her head, but that wasn't happening. So, she lay there and wondered if she was just having a bad dream. One that when she woke up would disappear into the subconscious, never to be thought of again.

The ceiling was white, the walls were white, and there was noise, she could definitely hear a lot of noise. Someone was crying, weeping really. Who was it? It sounded familiar. Her mother maybe? It wasn't Nicky though, where was she? She tried to speak, but she wasn't quite sure if she had said it out loud. God, this was tiring.

~E&F~

Lucy Owen was just 23 years old as she stood by the graveside of Nicola Abigale Jackson, supported by two crutches and her parents. She had been 19 years old when they had first met, 20 years old when they had first kissed, and 22 years old when they had last kissed. Her birthday had been just weeks ago, and it had passed by like any other day. She had received cards and flowers from well-wishers and fans, but with all the cards and flowers from the accident, none of them stood out as anything special; there was no happy birthday girlfriend card like there had been the year before.

The card had been a happy birthday darling wife one, but Nicky had crossed out the word "wife" and written "girlfriend" instead. She smiled as she remembered that, and then she cried when she remembered there would be no more.

She thought back to when her doctors had explained it was a miracle she was even alive. The police had been equally amazed that she had lived; she had been sitting in the area of the bus that had had the biggest impact and where everyone else had not made it.

She had stared at herself in the mirror. Bruises that had been deep purples, blue and black, now just a sallow yellow and orange. They were everywhere, and it was obvious that at one time she would have been a horrific sight to look at. Stitches marked a zipper down her face. She hadn't dared to even look at the rest of her body; her face was awful enough. One leg had been trapped in a cage-like contraption, screws drilled into her bones, holding it all together.

There wasn't a minute of the day that she wasn't in some form of pain. The physical pain she could numb; drugs could do a lot for a person like her. The emotional anguish was a different story. She pleaded to be sedated. The only time she didn't dream of them was when she was anesthetised. Her only solace from the torture of it all was when she went under the knife to fix one part of her or another. Skin grafts, bone reconstructions. She would pray not to wake up, but each time she would come around, still breathing. In the end, she realised that death was too easy. She wasn't supposed to die, that much was now obvious. She was meant to live. To live forever with the knowledge that she was the reason that Nicky was dead. It was her fault, and the pain of knowing that would be her penance.

Forget it

She had stood by the gravesides of four others too. Scott, Ben, Sarah, and Mikey. She had missed every funeral. She hadn't even known about them; goodbyes from her had had to wait. Her hospital stay had been two days shy of eight weeks.

She had 168 stitches, 23 of them down the left side of her face. A punctured lung, ruptured spleen, four broken ribs, and a leg broken in two places had meant for the first three weeks she hadn't even been conscious. The families of the deceased had waited long enough to bury their loved ones, and so Lucy had missed them. The press had been to them, well they went to Scott, Ben, Sarah, and Mike's. They printed nice little back stories about each of them and added photos of them and the flowers at the funerals. Nobody went to Nicky's, she was of no interest to the media, not until afterwards when they got wind of the lesbian angle and then they wanted to know everything.

For Lucy, it was the end.

Solar Flare was no more. Nicola Jackson was no more, and that meant that Lucy Owen was no more.

You can buy Escape and Freedom in full here:
http://getbook.at/Escapeandfreedom

Escape and Freedom will also be available in audiobook this summer!

The Doll Maker
A Sophie Whitton Story

Prologue

He hadn't grown up *knowing* that he would murder another person, let alone several, but he had. Hadn't everybody considered doing it? Only he had actually done it, and now it was all that consumed him. The small voice in his head grew louder with every passing day, soothing his worries, whispering encouragement and prodding him forwards.

It wasn't as grisly as the movies made out. There was blood, of course, but it hadn't been the stomach-curdling event that he thought it would be. Blind rage would do that for you. Or maybe he was just different, unaffected.

Thinking back to the moment when it first came down to it, he knew it was meant to be. He understood that as he took in the artistry of his creation, but it wasn't quite right. He was still working on that part. Funny, how it had just come to him like that. Just a flicker of a memory and he had the perfect accessory.

It was 9:04. A.M. when it happened; he knew that because he had looked at his watch just seconds before she had started. He just wanted to read the newspaper, but her voice shrieking across the room like a drunken banshee had grated on him. It went through him like nails down a chalkboard. He cocked his head at her, and right then, in that precise moment, he knew he would kill her. He knew it like he knew the sky was blue and grass was green. It was that simple.

In the background he could hear the faint echoes of a Whitney Houston song playing on the radio. Remnants of snow lingered outside through the cracked window pane. Winter had come late this year. He felt the hard, wooden floor beneath his feet, threadbare carpets doing little to cushion his steps. When he looked at her again, it wasn't *her* face that gawped back at him, reminding him why it was that she preferred his absence. She had friends coming over; she didn't want him hanging around tonight. The same excuses. It used to be because he was too young; now it was because he was too old.

He moved with such speed that she didn't even register the change in him. Too busy with her own selfish need to enjoy the pleasures in life to be concerned with him, and that was when he knew why he would kill her: because she reminded him of her. His mother.

His fist was first to react. A direct hit between the eyes, smashing the bridge of her nose in a bone-crunching blow. She staggered, but the bitch held firm, numb from the booze and drugs that consumed her. Her expression at first was quizzical when he grabbed her by the throat. As he began to squeeze, then she knew. He saw the fear within her. Her eyes bulging, his grip tightening.

"It's all your fault," he hissed, spittle bathing her face as he pulled her closer to him. "You and your filthy, vile and disgusting lifestyle-" His grip loosened a little. He would take his time. Anger was pushing him onwards, but hate would make this worthwhile. "-without you and him," he snarled at the thought of his father. "Without you both, she would still be here."

"Please, baby don't. Come on, I'll do anything." Her voice was scratchy as she gasped for every breath, to no avail. He remembered pleading similarly as a child not to be sent away; to no avail either. "Anything you want," she tugged at her top, showing him her tits; he liked her tits. He let go of her throat then and for a second she thought maybe, it would be okay. Until he slapped her. His palm hard against her cheek.

"You made her do it." His fingers wrapped around her scrawny neck once more. She had no idea what he was talking about as she clawed at his arms. His face contorted with a mix of rage and sadness, his eyes brimming with tears. "Because of you, she did it," he half-whispered, half-sobbed as his fingers gripped tighter.

The blackness came for her, as she knew it would. Her entire life she had lived with the blackness, the dark side of existence engulfing her before she had even had a chance at life. She had never thought it would come from someone like him though. He had adored her, fucked her because he wanted to, not because he was paying, though there were times he had paid for something more 'special.' There were many times under a man that she considered how her life would end. While they paid to thrust into her, she would take her mind elsewhere. Her thoughts would start off light: the idea of escaping it all, the addictions and the lifestyle that came with them, but eventually her thoughts would move towards the end. Her death would be lonely. Forgotten easily.

Afterwards, when he was finished with her, when she was displayed just the way he wanted her, he set about finishing the work.

The doll would be a reminder when they eventually found her.

You can buy The Doll Maker in full here:
http://getbook.at/TheDollMaker

37878848R00153

Made in the USA
Lexington, KY
01 May 2019